TRUSTING THE (

Riverbend, Texas Heat 1

Marla Monroe

MENAGE EVERLASTING

Siren Publishing, Inc.
www.SirenPublishing.com

A SIREN PUBLISHING BOOK
IMPRINT: Ménage Everlasting

TRUSTING THE COWBOYS
Copyright © 2012 by Marla Monroe

ISBN: 978-1-62241-256-3

First Printing: August 2012

Cover design by Les Byerley
All art and logo copyright © 2012 by Siren Publishing, Inc.

Printed in the U.S.A.

PUBLISHER
Siren Publishing, Inc.
www.SirenPublishing.com

TRUSTING THE COWBOYS

Riverbend, Texas Heat 1

MARLA MONROE
Copyright © 2012

Chapter One

Jared and Quade walked into the diner at a quarter to three, intent on a piece of Mattie's apple pie and coffee. It wasn't until they sat down in their usual spot that Jared noticed a new face. It looked like Mattie had finally found a waitress to take the place of Sandra. The other woman had quit to marry Jim and Mike Parham a little over a month ago. Mattie and her husbands had been making do ever since.

Quade, his friend and business partner, glanced his way. Evidently he had seen her, as well. A spark of interest lit up his eyes. Jared hadn't seen that look in his friend's face in a long time. Neither of them had been very sociable in the last few months. Keeping up with the ranch took most of their time, but more than that, they just hadn't met anyone who stirred their blood enough to make the effort.

The pretty waitress had long red hair pulled back in a ponytail. Even from there, he could tell she had the hourglass figure he and Quade preferred on a woman. Neither man liked the model stick figures that women seemed to strive to achieve. They liked to be able to hold on to a woman and not be afraid they were going to break her in half. Both he and Quade were big men, standing well over six feet. Quade, at six feet five, was two inches taller than he was.

He watched the red-headed beauty as she served coffee to Elmer and his missus. She had a heart-shaped face with a perky nose and pale blue eyes. He figured she was somewhere around five feet five inches. Short for them, but she made up for it in beauty. Her shapely body was hidden under a pair of loose-fitting jeans and a baggy T-shirt. Still, it didn't hide her ample breasts or womanly curves.

"Wonder who she is?" Quade leaned back in his chair and perused the woman up and down.

"She has a name tag on. When she walks over to get our order we can see."

The shapely woman grabbed another coffee pot and two cups before making her way to their table. As she drew nearer, Jared could see that she had several bruises on her arm, just below the sleeve of her T-shirt. They looked like they had been made by someone's fingers. Anger immediately rolled through him.

As if sensing his feelings, she took a step back. Then she firmed her shoulders and walked up to the table. She set the cups on the table.

"Would you like coffee?"

Quade read off her name tag. "Sure would, Lexie."

She nodded and poured their coffee before setting the pot on the table and pulling out her notepad.

"What can I get you?" Her voice sounded like soft music.

"We want a piece of Mattie's apple pie if there's any left," Jared told her.

"You're just in time to claim the last two pieces." She smiled as she picked up the coffee pot and turned to go.

"Thanks, darling." Quade was laying it on thick.

Jared flashed an amused smile at his partner.

"What?"

"You're already flirting."

"Doesn't hurt to flirt a little bit. At least until we know if she has a boyfriend. She's not wearing a wedding band."

Jared shook his head. "You work fast."

Lexie walked back toward them with two pieces of the apple pie and set them on the table in front of them.

"Anything else?" she asked.

Jared couldn't stop himself. He reached out and touched just above the bruises with his finger.

"You could tell me how you got these."

A flicker of unease flashed across her face and then was gone.

"Oh, I'm clumsy. I ran into the door trying to get ready for work. I bruise easily." She quickly turned on her heel and walked back to the counter where she and Mattie discussed something before she disappeared in the back.

"Those were fucking fingerprints on her arm, weren't they?" Quade obviously hadn't noticed them until Jared pointed them out.

"Yeah, that would be my guess."

"It couldn't have been anyone who came in here. Not unless it was a stranger. Mattie's husbands wouldn't have tolerated it." Quade stabbed at his pie.

Jared agreed with him. In Riverbend, Texas, women weren't accosted under any circumstance.

"You know the likelihood that she has a boyfriend just went up," Jared pointed out.

"I know, but he's an asshole. She deserves better than someone who abuses her."

Jared sighed. Quade had already made up his mind about her. He wanted her. It wasn't that Jared didn't. It was that they didn't know anything about her, and she was obviously a stranger in town. That meant she didn't know about the area's proclivity toward ménage relationships. He wondered how she felt about Mattie's two husbands. Did she even know about them yet?

She walked back over a few minutes later to refill their coffee.

"Can I get you anything else?" she asked.

"Your phone number," Quade said without missing a beat.

"Ah, I'm seeing someone but thanks for asking." She ducked her head and hurried over to the counter where she busied herself cleaning it.

"Well, now you know." Jared grinned at his partner.

"Doesn't mean anything. She didn't look happy about being with him. I plan on romancing her and luring her away from the asshole."

"You're playing with fire, buddy."

"I want her. She's special. Did you see how she smiled earlier? And she has a body made for loving, not hurting."

"I'm not arguing with you. I want to bury my face between her breasts, but that's not likely to happen as long as she's already in a relationship. Are you a home wrecker now, Quade?"

"Not much of a home if he's abusing her," he said with a frown.

"Maybe it was an accident and she's deliriously happy with him."

"Maybe, and maybe not. I aim to find out." Quade stood up and threw some bills on the table then walked out.

Jared huffed out a breath and stood up to pay the tab. When he walked over to the register, it was Mattie who checked him out.

"How was everything?" she asked with a beaming smile.

"You know your pie was delicious. We don't have to tell you that."

"Then why did Quade storm out?" She had a thoughtful expression on her face.

"What can you tell me about your new waitress?"

Jared saw her eyes twinkle.

"She's a sweet girl. Has a bastard of a boyfriend. He works over at the junkyard outside of town, when he works."

"She love him?" Jared asked.

"I think she's scared to death of him. She has bruises all over her. She's only been here a little over a week so far. I don't know much else about her. They moved here a little over two weeks ago."

"Thanks, Mattie. See you later." Jared walked outside the little diner and looked around for Quade.

He saw him talking to Will Hughes at the barbershop. Since he knew his partner wasn't about to get a haircut, he must be pumping the gossip mill for information. He was determined to find out more about her, that was for sure. Now everyone in town would know he was interested in her. Quade knew that, and it obviously didn't matter to him.

Will waved as he walked up. "Hey there, Jared. How are you?"

"Doing fine, Will. How about you and your family?"

"We're all healthy. The boys are driving their mom crazy. Terrible twos and all."

"Quade, you ready to head back to the ranch?"

"Yeah, need to see about the heifers still calving. Can't believe we have two this late in the season."

"Quade tells me you're interested in the new girl working over at the diner. She's got a real piece of work for a boyfriend. I'd be careful if I was you."

"What do you mean?" Jared didn't like the sound of that.

"He's a bully. He hasn't hit her in public, or you know someone would have put a stop to it, but she has bruises all over her arms. I don't like the bastard."

"Let us know if you hear anything concerning them," Quade said.

"Will do. I take it you're still interested. Things like this can backfire on you, you know. She might be in love with him and not take kindly to you interfering."

"Thanks for the warning, but I don't think so. We'll see you around." Quade shook his hand then headed for the truck.

Jared caught up with him and shook his head. "I hope you know what you're doing, Quade."

"Are you going to tell me that you can stand around and let him treat her like that?" Quade stopped with his hand on the door handle and turned to stare at him.

Jared ran his hand through his hair. "No, but heading in full blast isn't the way to go about it. We need more information first to know where things stand between them. Then we act."

Jared wasn't sure when he had made up his mind to make her theirs, but somewhere between the diner and the barbershop, the decision was made. Now he hoped he didn't regret it.

* * * *

Lexie waited until the two hunky men had walked out of the diner before returning to the counter. Mattie flashed her a knowing look and patted her hand.

"They're real good men, Lexie. You don't have to be afraid of them. They would never lay a hand on a woman in anger."

"Why are you telling me this?" she asked.

"Because you need someone who'll be good to you, not knock you around."

Lexie gasped and wrapped her arms around herself. She had no idea Mattie was so intuitive. But then Lowery hadn't been all that subtle about what he thought of her when he had been in the diner during the last week. One day he had even slapped her in the truck before letting her out to go to work. She had been sure everyone would know, but when she looked in the mirror, both cheeks were red in embarrassment. Either no one had seen him hit her, or they didn't care.

"He's all I have, Mattie. I can't afford to leave him." There, she'd said it. She had let someone know that she wasn't happy living with the man.

"You can walk out anytime you want, Lexie. There's a shelter here in town that takes in anyone without a place to stay." The woman disappeared in the back.

Lexie wasn't sure what to think. She knew if she tried to leave him he would come after her. She didn't want anyone else to get hurt because of her, but dear God she was tired of dealing with him. Nothing she did was good enough or fast enough. Sex was only an excuse to hurt and humiliate her further.

All during the remainder of her shift, Lexie's thoughts bounced around in her head about the possibility of leaving him. At ten that night, Lowery walked in with his usual scowl and plopped down at the counter.

"You ready to go?"

"Just about. I need to finish filling the napkin holders. Then I'll be ready."

"Hurry your ass up. You should have had that done by now. You know I'm ready to go home when I get here." He smelled of booze.

"I don't actually get off till ten thirty, Lowery."

"Don't argue with me. Now get me some coffee."

Lexie emptied the last of the coffee into a cup and passed it to him. Then she quickly escaped to the back to wash out the pot.

"Are you okay, Lexie?" Mike asked.

Mike was the evening short-order cook who locked up when Lexie left at night. He was working his way through college by working nights and weekends at the diner.

"I'm fine. He's grumpy tonight."

"Seems like he's always grumpy to me," Mike said.

"Lexie! Get your ass out here." Lowery's voice boomed from out front.

She hurried through the door to the front counter, wiping her hands on her apron.

"What's wrong?"

"Are you in there flirting with that kid? Don't you have any pride in yourself? I ought to wring your neck. You throw yourself at every cock that walks by."

Lexie cringed. He was winding up to be in a foul mood tonight.

"I'm not flirting, Lowery. He's got a steady girlfriend. They're planning to get married after college."

He raised his hand but lowered it when Mike walked out of the back.

"Get your stuff and let's go." Lowery stood up and stuck his hands on his hips.

Lexie gave Mike a watery smile before returning to the back to clock out and grab her things. She didn't want to go home with Lowery in the mood he was in. It would be bad. At least she wouldn't be coming back to work for two days. It would give her time to heal.

She hurried through the door, with Lowery stomping behind her. When she reached the passenger side of the truck, she reached for the door handle only to have her hair jerked so that she lost her balance and fell back into Lowery's arms.

"Think you're going to get away with flirting right in front of me? Just wait until I get you home. You'll learn who you belong to if it's the last thing I do." He shoved her face-first into the door and slapped the back of her head before walking around to the driver's side.

Lowery yelled and cursed at her all the way to the tiny trailer they rented just outside of town. She tuned him out and thought long and hard about trying to leave him again. The last time he'd found her and nearly put her in the hospital. The worst part of it was that he'd hurt the guy who'd helped her find another place to live. She didn't want anyone else to suffer because of her.

Lexie thought about the extra tip money hidden away in her shoe. If he knew she was holding out on him, he'd probably kill her. She needed the money, though, in order to get a place of her own, and she needed it for the bus to get away so he wouldn't find her again. That was where she had made her first mistake, staying in the same town. She wouldn't do that again.

They pulled into the drive of the dilapidated trailer, and Lowery cut the engine. She hurried out of the truck but had to wait for him to unlock the door to the trailer. Before she had even crossed the threshold, Lowery shoved her to the floor and kicked her. She balled up, protecting her face and stomach, knowing she had to be able to work her next shift in two days. If she had a black eye, people would talk, and Lowery didn't like it when people talked about him. And she didn't like it when Lowery was upset.

Chapter Two

Saturday evening, Jared and Quade drove into town for a beer and to shoot the breeze with their friends from neighboring ranches. It had been a long two days since they had been to town, punctuated by birthing difficult claves and rounding up stray cattle. They had three ranch hands, but it took all of them sometimes to keep the ranch running smoothly.

Quade was looking forward to this trip to town for more than one reason. He planned to see that pretty waitress from the diner again. He hoped she was working tonight. If she wasn't, he would find out where she lived. *And do what? You can't barge in where she lives and ask her out.* Quade huffed out a breath and climbed out of the truck.

"You heading to the diner or to get a beer first?" Jared gave him a knowing smile.

"Beer first. I figured we would catch her getting off work and talk to her."

"Good idea. Let's go see if someone knows any more about her than what we do." Jared led the way to the local bar.

Once inside, they made their way to the bar through the already dense crowd and held up their hands for beers. The bartender, Harold Brewster, smiled and nodded at them. Harold and his brother Humphrey were married to Cindy. Humphrey was an accountant and had an office in town.

"What's going on, boys? Haven't seen you in here in a month of Sundays," Harold bellowed out.

Quade and Jared took their beers and filled the bartender in on the woes of a rancher's life.

"Yeah, and you love every minute of it." Harold laughed and moved back down the bar to tend to his customers.

"Hey, Quade, Jared. How are you?" Nate, one of Mattie's husbands, stuck out his hand.

"Hey, Nate. How are you doing? Mattie working?" Quade looked around for the woman.

"No, with the new girl, Mattie is taking more time off again. Come on over and join us. I think she wants to talk to you two about something."

Jared's brows furrowed. Quade wondered what Mattie wanted with them. They followed Nate over to where the woman was sitting with her other husband, Bruce. She immediately brightened when she saw them heading her way.

"Just who I need to see. Sit down, you two."

They shook hands with Bruce and then took a seat.

"Hey, Mattie. How are you doing?" Jared waggled his eyebrows at her. "Finally thinking about letting us whisk you away to our place?"

"Don't make me get in your face, Jared," Bruce said with a laugh.

"You guys." She fluttered her hand at them. "I want to talk to you about Lexie."

"What about Lexie?" Quade was immediately all business.

"Are you really interested in her, or are you just making time?" Bruce asked before Mattie did.

"We're serious about her. Why?" Quade stared at Bruce.

"Because if you're just wanting to get into her pants, she doesn't need more crap. She's got enough to deal with without you making it worse." Mattie poked Bruce in the ribs.

He scowled at her but kissed the top of her head anyway.

"What's going on?" Jared asked cautiously.

"Mike said her boyfriend was a bit rough with her the other night. Then when she came in this afternoon she was walking funny, like she was in pain. When I asked her about it, she said she was fine, just stove-up from cleaning while she was off work. I don't believe it, though. I think she's hurt."

Quade immediately jumped up, but both Jared and Bruce stood up with him, keeping him from taking off for the diner.

"Easy there, big boy." Bruce placed a hand on Quade's shoulder. "We need to talk about this before anyone goes off half-cocked."

Quade sat back down, scowling at the other men. He didn't want to do any more talking. He needed to see about Lexie. It briefly occurred to him that he hadn't spoken more than a dozen words to her and already he was half in love with her. Something about her called to him. Never mind that as a man he detested crimes against women in general.

"Mike said Lowery got angry because he thought she was flirting with him. He swears there was no flirting, and I believe him," Mattie said. "The thing is, if you interfere, you could make things worse on her. If you're not planning on this being more than a few weeks of fun, don't get involved with her."

"Are we through talking yet?" Quade asked with a growl.

"Quade, don't talk like that to Mattie." Bruce leaned forward.

"I'm sorry, Mattie. I don't mean any disrespect. I just know Lexie is waiting for that good-for-nothing asshole to pick her up, and there is no telling what he'll do to her tonight."

"She doesn't get off till ten thirty, so you have time," Nate assured him.

Quade sighed and relaxed slightly against the back of the chair. He needed to regain control of himself, or he would scare her for sure. Jared nodded at him as if he knew what he was thinking. No doubt if anyone knew, it would be Jared. They went all the way back to grade school. Quade's family had been poor white trash living in a rundown shack near Jared's ranch. His old man worked for them when he was sober and beat on him and his mom when he wasn't. There were many days he went to school black and blue.

Jared hadn't cared that Quade's family was poor. He had befriended Quade and taught him how to ride and how to be a boy. As soon as he was big enough, he went to work for Jared's father and took his old man's place. The bastard rarely showed up to work anyway. So it fell to Quade to be the man of the house while his dad slowly drank himself to death.

When Quade turned seventeen, his father had died of alcohol poisoning. His mom died two years later of cancer. Quade moved in with Jared's family, and when the old Bartwell ranch went up for sale, the two men had pooled their money from working the ranch and riding in local rodeos to buy the run-down place. Now, at the ripe old age of thirty, they were self-sufficient and known for their superior beef.

When Jared's parents had decided to retire to Arizona where the weather was dry and warm, they took over their ranch and merged it with their own. Now they had one of the larger ranches in the region.

"How do you know her boyfriend won't go to pick her up early?" Quade asked.

"Because he's right over there tying one on." Bruce pointed the bastard out to them.

"He's name is Lowery, and from what Harold says he spends most of his nights here." Nate shook his head in disgust. "He's usually pretty wasted when he leaves."

"Not too wasted to beat on Lexie, though," Quade pointed out.

"Maybe we should go talk to her while he's busy," Jared said.

"I like that idea." Quade stood up after downing the last of his beer.

"Just remember what I said," Mattie pointed out. "If you're not going to take care of her for more than a few weeks, don't mess with her. She's been through enough."

"You don't worry about her anymore, Mattie. She's under our protection as soon as we get her away from that asshole." Quade made his way through the crowd, passing within spitting distance of Lowery as he did.

Once they were outside the bar, they drove over to the diner and parked. Jared touched his shoulder.

"Remember to relax and try not to scowl at her. She's not going to be real trusting of anyone."

Quade nodded and drew in a deep breath. All he could think about was closing his fingers around the neck of the bastard who'd hurt her. He had to make an effort to calm down.

By the time they walked into the diner at a quarter of ten, Quade was much calmer. He watched Lexie grab two cups and the coffeepot as they took a set at the counter.

"Coffee?" she asked.

"Sounds good." Quade smiled at her.

Lexie smiled back then sobered up and schooled her features.

"What can I get you?" she asked, all business.

"Any pie left?" Jared asked.

"Um, there's apple and a piece of lemon meringue left."

"I'll have the apple," Jared said.

"Give me the lemon." Quade watched as she moved back to where the pies were.

She did limp, and she favored her left side. Add to that the fact that she was wearing long sleeves on a hot May night was all he needed to know. She was hurting.

"Here you go. I'll check back to see if you need more coffee in a few minutes." She slipped back to the back with the empty coffeepot.

"She's hurting, Jared."

"Yeah, I can see. How do you plan to approach her?"

"Straight up. She's not going to trust anyone that hedges."

When she returned to make another pot of coffee, Jared called her over.

"I know you told us before that you were seeing someone, but we hoped that maybe you would leave him and let us take care of you."

"Both of you?" she squeaked out.

"Yeah, both of us."

"Um, thanks, but I'm really not looking for another relationship."

"We know he hurts you, Lexie. Let us help you get away from him." Quade had to try.

"I've got a plan. I'm going to leave him next week when the bus comes through town. I have almost enough money now, so I'll have it by then." She smiled.

"Honey, let us help you now. He's already hurt you bad enough that you can't walk straight." Quade couldn't stand the idea of her going back to him for even one night, much less three or four.

"I'm fine." She lifted her chin and returned to the coffeemaker. She fiddled with it, setting it up to brew.

Quade looked at Jared. His friend shook his head. There wasn't anything they could do to help her if she didn't want their help. It was tearing him up inside, but he wasn't one to beg. Instead, he dropped a large tip on the counter and nodded at Jared that it was time to go.

They walked out of the diner about the time that Lowery pulled his beat-up pickup into the parking lot. Jared shook his head when Quade started to head toward the man.

"Don't start something. It will only get her into more trouble."

Quade knew he was right, but it didn't make him feel any better. He would think about it some more and come up with another idea. There had to be a way to convince her to give them a try.

* * * *

Quade stretched. He and Jared had been working on fences all morning. He was ready for something decent to eat besides their cooking.

"Let's head in to town and get lunch. I'm sick of sandwiches, and neither one of us can cook worth crap."

"You're just wanting to see Lexie again," Jared teased.

"And you don't?"

"Hell yeah, I do, but I was waiting on you to give in first."

"Asshole." Quade grinned and headed for the shower.

The diner would be clearing out by the time they got there. It would give them a little more privacy to try and win her over to their side. He'd been thinking about it a lot while they were working on the fence line. They needed someone to cook for them. She could be their cook, and that would give her a reason to live there until they could convince her to be their wife.

With a plan firmly sketched out in his mind, Quade and Jared climbed into the cab of the truck and headed for town. It was two thirty when they pulled into the parking lot. There were two other trucks still there.

Mattie greeted them with a strained smile on her face.

"Hey, you two. Decided you needed something good to eat for lunch?"

"You know we can't cook worth crap, Mattie. What's for lunch today?"

Mattie went over the special then waited for them to order. Once they had finished, Quade looked around for Lexie.

"I wonder if she's in the back."

"She may not be here yet. We don't know what her hours are." Jared looked around as well.

Mattie returned a few minutes later with iced tea.

"Where's Lexie?" Quade asked.

"She was supposed to be her at two thirty, but she hasn't made it yet."

"Is she usually late?" Jared asked.

"If she walks she is a couple of minutes sometimes but not much later."

Quade looked at his watch. It was two thirty-eight. Not really that late yet.

"If she isn't here in another ten minutes, we'll go see about her," Jared said.

Mattie nodded. "I'd send Bruce, but he's the only one I have here besides me today. Mike had to study for one of his finals."

"We'll see about her, Mattie."

As soon as they got their meal, they wolfed it down and gave up waiting on her. It was nearly three now. Quade didn't like it.

"Mattie, call the sheriff and ask him to meet us at her house. I don't have a good feeling about this," Jared said.

"Let's go, Jared." Quade walked out of the diner and climbed into the driver's side of the truck.

After getting directions from Mattie, they made it to the trailer in less than five minutes. It would have been a good twenty-minute walk to the diner from there. The windows were all dark with curtains pulled tight. There wasn't a truck in the drive, so Lowery was gone. Just as they opened their doors to climb out, the sheriff pulled up and got out. He shook his head at them.

"What in the hell are you two getting into here?"

"Lexie didn't show up for work today. The last time we saw her she was walking with a limp and had bruises on her arms," Quade said. "I think something's wrong."

"Let me handle this, guys." He walked over to the trailer door and knocked on it. The door opened with his knock.

He looked back at Quade and Jared and drew his gun.

"Lexie? Are you in there? It's Sheriff Tidwell. I'm coming in, Lexie."

He eased the door open and disappeared into the trailer. Quade wasn't waiting around. He followed the sheriff, with Jared right behind him.

"Fuck!"

Quade immediately hurried into the room where the sheriff had disappeared. Lying on the floor between the bedroom and the bathroom was Lexie, naked and all curled up in a ball. There were bruises all over her body, some in the shape of shoeprints on her back.

"I need an ambulance out at the trailer park outside of town where my car is parked, Lettie. Now!" Sheriff Tidwell used his radio as he knelt beside Lexie's still body.

"Aw, hell. Lexie, can you hear me?" Quade was afraid to touch her.

"Don't move her, Quade. We don't know if she has any spinal injuries. Let the paramedics see about her."

"Get a blanket to cover her, Jared." Quade looked up at his best friend. He had tears in his eyes.

They covered her up and waited for the ambulance to arrive.

Chapter Three

Lexie woke up with a headache, hurting all over. She immediately recognized where she was by the smell. She was in the hospital. How had she gotten there? God, her body hurt. Lowery had been furious when he found her money. She still couldn't believe he had stripped the bed. She had never known him to change a sheet in all the time that she had been with him.

She had stashed her money in a Ziploc bag under the box springs. What was he doing looking under the box springs?

She moaned and tried to turn over, but it hurt too much.

"Easy there, Lexie."

She knew that voice. Where did she know it from? She forced her eyes open all the way and saw the two men from the diner sitting at her bedside. Even through her blurry vision they were easy to look at. Mattie had told her who they were and that she could trust them, but she knew better than to trust anyone.

"What are you doing here?"

"We've been with you since the sheriff found you unconscious in that fucking trailer," Quade said.

"Where's Lowery?" She tried once again to move, but it was just too much for her.

"Don't move, Lexie," Jared, the other man said.

"He's in jail until he makes bail," Quade told her.

"He's going to be so pissed." She couldn't help the tears building up in her eyes.

"Shh. He can't hurt you. All you have to do is press charges. We'll take care of you." Quade slipped a strand of hair back behind her ear.

"He'll just get out, and then he'll be even worse. Oh, God. How did he find my money?" The tears slipped from her eyes.

"I don't want you worrying about him at all, Lexie. We're going to take care of you from now on. You have a home with us."

"Why would you get involved with me?" she demanded.

She knew that there would be only one reason. They wanted her for sex. That was all men ever wanted. Why had she ever trusted Lowery in the first place?

"We care about you, Lexie. Let us help you."

She swallowed. It hurt to do anything. He had really messed her up this time. Usually she ended up in the emergency room for a few hours and she was home again before he even showed back up. This time, it was bad. Her body ached all over. Her head felt as if a sledgehammer beat inside it.

"Will you let us help you, Lexie?" Quade asked.

"He'll hurt you if you help me."

"Honey, that asshole can't do a thing to us. Don't worry about us. We can handle ourselves," Jared told her.

There was a knock at the door, and a nurse walked in.

"Good, she's awake. Why don't you two step outside while I help her turn over and take care of her IV?"

"She's hurting. Can you give her something for pain?" Jared asked.

"I'll check with the doctor. It's only been five hours. I'm not sure he will want her to have anything with her head injury, but I'll ask."

They stepped outside the room while the nurse fussed over her.

"You've got some good-looking men worried about you. I hope you dump the asshole that did this to you." She helped Lexie turn to her side.

While she fiddled with the IV in her hand, the nurse kept up a steady stream of dialogue.

"They've been here from the beginning and haven't left your bedside except when I've made them so I could check on you. You're not, are you?"

"What?" Lexie couldn't remember what the question was.

"Going to go back to the one who did this to you."

"I don't have anywhere to go." Lexie couldn't help the tears that slid from her swollen eyes.

"I bet those men will take good care of you if you let them." The nurse patted her hand and opened the door to let them back in.

"Hey there, Lexie. Would you like something to drink?" Quade asked.

"No, thanks."

"Lexie, we want you to listen to us for a few minutes. Don't say anything until you've had time to hear us out, okay?" Jared sat on the chair next to the bed while Quade stood.

"We know you plan to leave Lowery, but you can't go anywhere until you're healed up. Why don't you move in with us? You can have your own room, and we'll pay you to cook for us. We can't cook worth anything and don't have time to go to town every day for meals."

"Why would you help me? You don't even know me," she whispered.

"We care about you. We want the chance to get to know you. If when you've saved enough to start over you still want to leave, we'll help you get to wherever you want to go." Quade didn't appear to like saying that.

"I don't know. I can't think right now."

"Just think about it when you feel better. We're not going to change our minds, and you've got plenty of time to rest." Quade bent over the bed and kissed her lightly on the forehead.

The nurse hurried back into the room. "I talked to the doctor. He said all you can have is some Tylenol, honey. You can have something stronger once he's sure your concussion isn't serious."

She helped Lexie take the Tylenol with a sip of water and then left them once again.

"Try to go back to sleep, baby. One of us will be here with you until you get out of the hospital. We're not leaving you alone," Jared told her.

She nodded and closed her eyes once again. Once her head settled down some form the Tylenol, she managed to drift off into sleep.

* * * *

The sheriff arrived several hours later to talk to Lexie. They went down to the cafeteria for some coffee while they talked. Jared really didn't like leaving her alone but planned to be back before the other man left.

"She's in a lot of pain, man. I can't stand it." Quade ran a hand through his hair before settling his hat back on his head.

"Another few hours and the doctor said she could have something stronger. Maybe she'll sleep the rest of the time till then. You going to be okay to stay with her while I check on the ranch?" Jared asked.

"Yeah. I'll be fine. Make sure her room is ready for when we take her home. I don't want her to have to worry about anything."

"She hasn't agreed yet," Jared pointed out with a smile.

"She will." Quade took a drink of the coffee and grimaced.

"You ready to head back?" Jared asked after a few minutes.

"Yeah. This stuff tastes like crap. Bring me a cup of coffee from the diner when you come back tomorrow."

"I will." He shook his head.

Quade lived for his coffee. They had a Keurig machine at the ranch, and Quade kept it busy. Jared ordered their coffee online since the stores in town didn't stock the K-Cups for the machine. He wondered what sort of coffee Lexie liked or if she preferred tea. The machine made hot tea as well as hot chocolate.

They walked back to the room and knocked on the door. The sheriff opened the door with a grim expression.

"What's wrong?" Quade asked.

"She's scared of him. She doesn't want to press charges because she has nowhere else to go."

"Lexie. We told you we want you to move out to the ranch. You'll be safe there, and we need a cook. Press charges and let us help you do what you want to do. Doesn't matter what it is, you can do it." Jared pleaded with her.

"Even if I want to leave in a few months?" she asked.

"Even if," Quade told her.

"All right. I'll press charges."

The sheriff smiled and had her sign her name at the bottom of the complaint. Jared couldn't help but notice how bad she shook when she did. Her arms were covered in bruises. God, he wanted a few minutes alone with that son of a bitch.

He felt Quade relax slightly at her agreement. He patted his friend's shoulder. They had a chance with her now. All they had to do was go slow, treat her well, and keep her safe. Hopefully the asshole would move on after he finally got out of jail.

After the sheriff left, Jared talked to her some about the ranch. She seemed genuinely interested.

"You'll like it out there, Lexie. It's quiet, and there's plenty of room for you to explore if you want to."

"What do you like to eat? I'll be cooking for you, so I need to know what you like."

"Anything you cook, Lexie," Quade assured her with a smile. "You have no idea just how bad our cooking is."

She smiled then grimaced when it pulled her busted lip. "I'm not a chef or anything, but I can cook basic meals."

"That's all we need," Jared said with a smile.

"I need to get my things from the trailer. I don't want to go by myself."

"Tell you what. When you get out of here, we'll go with you so you won't be by yourself." Quade gently patted her head.

"I've got to go, Lexie. Quade will be here with you tonight. I'll be back in the morning. I'm bringing him some coffee. Do you want anything?"

She smiled but shook her head slightly. "No thanks."

"I'll see you tomorrow when they tell us you can come home. Okay?"

"Okay."

Jared walked out of the room with Quade behind him.

"I'll call you as soon as the doctor says she can leave. I want to be sure we get her things from the trailer before the asshole gets out on bail. Without her to post it, hopefully he won't be able to anytime soon."

"Keep her safe and get some rest. I have a feeling it's going to be a rough few days."

"You're probably right," Quade said.

"I'll see you tomorrow." Jared waited until Quade walked back into the hospital room before leaving.

On the way back to the ranch, he thought about what he needed to do when he got there. It was nearly ten. He needed to check in with the hands and ready the master bedroom for Lexie. It hadn't been used since they built the new house. They had always planned to find a woman to share. Jared's parents lived in a ménage relationship, and most of the town of Riverbend, Texas had ménage or polyamorous relationships.

He and Quade had shared women between them off and on over the years. It was just a forgone conclusion they would marry a woman together one day. Now that they had found the woman they were looking for, it was time to get the bedroom ready. He could hardly wait to see her sleeping in their bed.

Jared pulled into the drive to find one of the hands waiting on him on the front porch.

"Something wrong?" he demanded as soon as he stepped out of the truck.

"No, nothing major. I just figured I'd save you a trip out to the bunkhouse. The calf we were worried about seems to be eating better, but he's still shaky on his legs. I called the vet and asked him to come out and take a look at him in the morning. I hope that's okay."

"Yeah, that's a good call. I'll be here most of the day tomorrow. When they call me to come pick them up, I'll be gone for a couple of hours, and then we'll be back."

"So is it true? Have you two found your woman?"

"Yep, if we can convince her, that is."

"She's bound to realize you're going to treat her better than that good-for-nothing bastard she was with." The hand smiled.

"News travels fast," Jared said with a shake of his head.

"You know how cowboys are. We like a good gossip."

"I'll see you in the morning." Jared clapped the other man on the back before walking inside the house.

It was quiet inside. With Quade gone, it seemed downright morbid. He couldn't wait to have Lexie there to liven things up some. It would feel good to come in after a long day in the saddle to her and some home cooking.

Jared walked to the master bedroom and opened the double doors that closed it off from the rest of the house. The spare bedrooms were all upstairs while the master suite was downstairs behind the kitchen. He and Quade had bedrooms upstairs. She would have the run of the house when she got there, but he wanted the master bedroom to be comfortable for her. He checked to make sure there were plenty of towels in the bathroom.

He figured the first thing she would want to do when she got there was have a nice long soak in the bathtub. It was large enough for three people, as was the walk-in shower. The platform bed was custom made by the Mitchel twins. They made customized furniture and cabinets. They had been the ones who had helped them build this house several years ago.

Satisfied that the room was ready for her, Jared closed it back up and headed for his room. He needed to shower and get into bed. He had a full day ahead of him tomorrow.

Chapter Four

"Well, young lady. You're lucky to be alive. He did a number on you. You're going to be quite sore for several days. I want you to rest for twenty-four hours, and then you can get up and move around some." The doctor signed her paperwork and handed it over to the nurse. "As soon as they finish the discharge process, you can go. I hope I don't see you back in here again."

"I don't plan on it," she said.

Lexie shivered. Her body hurt all over, but at least her headache was a dull throb now. She could deal with that. The nurse told her she would be back to help her dress in a few minutes.

"Oh! I don't have any clothes!"

"I have something for you to wear," Quade told her. He handed her the sack.

"Mattie brought this for you yesterday. It's just a pair of warm-ups 'cause we didn't know your size."

"That was so thoughtful of her. I've really let her down." Lexie hung her head. She hated that she hadn't proven to be a good employee.

"She understands, Lexie. You can't be blamed for what that asshole did to you."

"I should have tried to leave him again sooner, but I needed the money to get away."

"Shh. Don't work yourself up over it. It's all in the past now. You're going to be fine, and you have your entire life ahead of you." Quade smiled at her.

He really was a handsome man. He was somewhere around six feet five, with massive muscles in his arms, and legs built like tree trunks. He had a broad shoulders and a wide chest that tapered down to a narrow waist and rounded hips. His dark brown hair was shaggy and needed a trim. She loved his eyes, though. They were a clear green that darkened when he was thinking.

Jared had short black hair with equally dark eyes. He had an easy smile that drew her to him as much as Quade's green eyes. He wasn't as muscular as Quade, and he wasn't as tall. Jared stood at about six feet three inches. He made her want to laugh, where Quade made her feel safe.

"I'm going to call Jared and let him know he can come pick us up." He picked up the phone and dialed a number.

"Hey, yeah, the doc just signed her discharge papers. The nurses are getting things ready now." Quade smiled over at Lexie as he talked to Jared.

Finally, he put the phone down and smiled at her. "Jared will be her in about thirty minutes to take us to get your things."

The nurse walked back in and lifted her eyebrows for Quade to leave. He handed over the bag of clothes and walked outside the room to wait.

"Let's get you into these clothes so you can go home now. Then I'll go over your paperwork about what you need to do."

The nurse helped her pull on the underwear and warm-ups before reviewing the doctor's orders with her. She reminded her to stay quiet for another twenty-four hours before doing anything.

She was sitting on the edge of the bed when Quade walked back in. He smiled at her and took her hand in his.

"We're going to help you pack up your things in case Lowery shows up. According to the sheriff, he made bail this morning. He isn't supposed to be around the trailer until this afternoon. The sheriff warned him off."

"He's going to be so mad, Quade."

"Don't worry about that. He can't hurt you ever again. We'll keep you safe."

Twenty minutes later, Jared walked in with a smile and a handful of daises. He presented them to Lexie with a flourish.

"Thank you." She smelled them and grinned. "I've never had flowers before."

Jared frowned. "Never?"

"No." She lifted her chin. She didn't want him feeling sorry for her.

"I feel bad now that I only picked them. I should have gotten you a real bouquet."

"No. They are perfect. I like wildflowers. They're natural." Lexie sighed and smiled at the man. He'd been trying to put her at ease.

"You ready to leave?"

"I'm ready. I hate hospitals."

Jared walked back out the door but returned in less than a second with a wheelchair.

"I can walk, Jared."

"It's required. I managed to talk the nurse into letting me wheel you out, though."

Quade helped her stand up and slip into the chair. Then he settled her feet onto the footrests. The trip out to the truck took less than a minute. The next thing she knew, she was sitting between the two men in the cab of the truck as they pulled out of the hospital parking lot.

She didn't say anything as they drove over to the trailer where she had been living for the last three weeks. She let Quade help her down from the truck. Then she followed as they walked over to the door. Jared knocked on the door. When no one answered, he pulled out a key and unlocked the door, much to Lexie's surprise. At her lifted brow, he smiled.

"I'm friends with the landlord. He let me borrow the key to get your things."

They walked into the trailer and the musty smell they got when they had been closed up for a few hours without the air on. They followed her into the bedroom, where she began to gather her few belongings. She had several changes of clothes and her toiletries all packed up in Walmart bags in less than ten minutes. She had so little to her name it was embarrassing. She swallowed down the tears. There was no use for them.

"Is that all? You sure nothing else here is yours?" Quade asked.

"No, the furniture came with the trailer, and all I had was my clothes."

"Let's get out of here, then." Jared took the bags, and Quade helped her back into the truck just as Lowery's truck pulled into the drive behind them.

"What the fuck are you doing in my home?" He climbed out of his truck and stomped over to where Quade had Lexie behind him.

"You're not supposed to be here until this afternoon, Lowery. The sheriff warned you to stay away from her." Jared stepped into Lowery's personal space and backed him up.

Lexie was afraid they were going to fight. She tried to edge around Quade to stop them, but Quade kept her firmly behind him.

"I have to protect what's mine. She's a little thief. She'll steal everything I have if I'm not here to watch her."

"That's not true." Lexie tried to walk around Quade again, but he wasn't letting her.

"Well, all she took was clothes, so nothing is missing," Jared told him. "Now back off and let us leave."

"She's nothing but trouble, anyway. You can't get her to do a damn thing. She can't keep one man satisfied. She sure as hell ain't going to be able to keep both of you happy. You'll see."

Lexie was humiliated. What would they think of her? She climbed into the cab of the truck and looked down at her hands as Quade climbed in after her. He fastened her seatbelt for her and wrapped an arm around her shoulders, careful of where she was sore.

Jared walked around the truck and climbed in. He pulled out over the side of the drive once he had the truck started. Then he headed toward the road leading to the other side of town.

"You okay, Lexie?" Jared asked in a soft voice.

"Yes. Thanks for going with me to get my things."

"There's no way you're ever going to be alone with that man again." Quade was holding her hand now. "He's dangerous, and you have no business around him."

"Believe me. I don't want to be around him ever again. He wasn't like that when I first met him."

"I know. He hid his true nature to get his hooks into you. Now forget about him. You've got the rest of your life ahead of you." Jared patted her leg.

Twenty minutes later, they pulled into the drive leading to their ranch. Lexie got her first glimpse of the two-story ranch house as they pulled into the front. There was a wraparound porch with rocking chairs and a swing. She would love to live in such a house. She followed them inside, where they promptly walked through the living room around to a small hall that led to a back room.

When Jared opened the double doors and showed her into the massive bedroom, her jaw flew open. Snapping it closed again, Lexie shook her head.

"I can't stay here. It's the master suite."

"It's right next to the kitchen, so it's perfect for you to be able to get in and out of the kitchen without a hassle. Plus, we live upstairs. We don't use this room. It has its own bathroom, too," Jared pointed out.

"It's not right."

"It's our house. We say what goes, Lexie. This is your room."

Quade sounded strange to her. She stared at him then sighed. They were right in that being next to the kitchen was the best place for her to be since she was the cook. Maybe it would be okay. They obviously hadn't been living in the room since there was a thin layer of dust everywhere, and the style was a little more feminine than masculine. She wondered who had decorated it. She liked it.

"Okay?" Quade asked.

"Okay. Only because it's next to the kitchen."

"Okay, Lexie. Let's get you situated. I'll let you unpack your things. Why don't you have a nice long soak in the tub to soothe those muscles? I know it will make you feel better." Jared showed her the bathroom. She quickly gasped then covered her mouth.

"It's wonderful. I've never seen a tub that big before."

"Glad you like it. Now you relax, and we'll check back with you in a little while."

They left her alone in the spacious master suite. Lexie just stood there for several seconds, trying to decide what to do. Finally, she sat on the bed and let the tears that had been threatening to fall all morning roll down her cheeks.

* * * *

Jared urged Quade out the door. He closed it behind them.

"Think she'll be okay in there alone?" Quade asked.

"She needs some space to take it all in, man. Give her time to adjust. She can't do anything for twenty-four hours according to the paperwork you showed me. She needs to relax and rest."

"What about Lowery? You know he is going to cause trouble. He isn't going to let her go without a fight." Quade's face took on a sneer.

"We'll warn the ranch hands about him and tell them that under no circumstances is he to be allowed on this land. I also think we should hire an extra hand to help out now. We need for one of us to be around her at all times."

"I agree," Quade said. "She's going to balk about one of us watching her all the time."

Jared grinned. Quade really was over his head in love with the woman. This was going to be equal parts fun and a pain.

"We don't dog her every step, Quade. We give her space, but one of us is in the house all the time with her. You can't hover over her, or you're going to scare her off. She's already afraid to be alone with anyone. Did you see how she kept looking at the door as if she might run through it at any moment?"

"Yeah. I guess you're right. I like being close to her, though."

"Back off, Quade, or you're going to fuck up."

His best friend nodded and huffed out a breath. "I think I'm going to go check on the ranch. You can watch out for her till dinner time."

"Got it covered. Let me know over the radio if there are any problems."

"Will do." Quade turned and walked out the back door toward the barn.

Jared ran a hand through his hair. Maneuvering them around each other was going to be like working a chest board with a five-year-old. He had his work cut out for him.

Realizing that they would probably need groceries, Jared started making a list. When he finished, he looked back over it and winced. Maybe he should let her make the grocery list. He was making it out like a bachelor who ate fast food.

He checked his watch and decided that Lexie had had enough time soaking. If she wasn't out of the tub by now, he would get her out. She didn't need to catch pneumonia in a tub full of cold water.

Jared knocked on the door but got no answer. He opened the door to find Lexie curled up on the bed wearing a pair of loose-fitting jeans and overly large T-shirt. He smiled. She needed to nap. He pulled the comforter over her then backed out of the room and returned to the kitchen. He fixed a cup of coffee. He loved sitting on the front porch looking out over the land. Maybe he would do that for awhile.

The ringing of the phone stopped him from going outside. Instead, he answered it and listened to what the sheriff had to say. It wasn't good. Lowery was a multitalented asshole. He had done time for anything from assault to drug charges. How had Lexie gotten mixed up with him? She seemed like such a sweet girl. The man had to have caught her at a bad time in her life to have pulled the wool over her eyes like he did.

The radio crackled, and Quade's voice sounded over the air.

"Go ahead."

"Everything seems fine out here. The cows are all close together for a change."

"Sounds good. What else?"

"I'm going to go ahead and check the west fence line again."

"Got your gun?"

"Always, Jared. I'll be careful. We haven't seen that mountain lion in months."

"Don't take any chances, Quade. We've got a woman to take care of now."

"Don't you worry. I'll be back by dinner time."

Jared hooked the radio back on his belt and walked out on the back porch to settle in a rocking chair. He would go back inside in a little while and start something for dinner.

Chapter Five

Lexie woke up stiff but not as sore as she had felt. For a few seconds, she was unsure where she was. Then the ranch and the beautiful bedroom rushed back to remind her. She sighed and looked over at the bedside table at the time. *Crap!* She needed to get in the kitchen if she was going to have dinner ready at a decent hour.

She stepped into her shoes and hurried down the hall to the kitchen, where she stopped to smile. It held all new stainless-steel appliances with granite countertops and an industrial-size fridge. She searched the pantry and the refrigerator to see what was available.

Not much outside of frozen dinners. I guess they really do need a cook.

She had just started dinner when Jared walked in from the back porch. He stared at her as if she had something on her nose.

"What?"

"You're not supposed to be in here. You're on bed rest for twenty-four hours."

"I can't stay in the bed that long. I'm fine. I need to move around or I'm going to be too stove-up to later. Besides, all I'm doing is throwing together something to eat. You don't have anything here to really cook with."

"Yeah, we need to get up a shopping list. I was hoping you could do that for me." Jared looked a little ashamed.

Lexie smiled despite her lip pulling at the split area. He was cute when he looked guilty.

"I'll make out a list when I get this done. You need to tell me what kind of foods you and Quade like."

"Honestly, anything that doesn't bite us first. We're not hard to please."

Lexie finished what she was doing and sat down to make out a grocery list. By the time she was finished, it was rather daunting. She hoped they didn't mind. There was very little in the form of staple goods.

She handed the list to Jared when he returned from answering a phone call. He looked over it and nodded.

"I think we need to add a little more meat and stock up the freezer some."

"That wouldn't hurt. You never know when you need an extra meal for some reason."

"Okay, now, back to bed. Just lie down for a little while. I'll keep an eye on the soup and call you when Quade gets back in."

"I really don't feel like lying back down," she grumbled.

Jared frowned. She sighed and retraced her steps back to the bedroom. She slipped out of her shoes and climbed up on the big, comfortable bed. Jared really seemed like a nice enough man. He hadn't really fussed at her or pushed her to do anything. Quite the opposite, he didn't seem to want her to do anything at all right now.

Lexie relaxed into the comforter and closed her eyes, thinking about the two men. They were so different. Where Jared was open and friendly, Quade was quiet and brooding. Still, they both had been nothing but kind to her and treated her like something precious. She had never been treated so sweetly.

She must have dozed after that, because a knock at the door sometime later jarred her awake.

"Lexie?"

"Yeah, come in." She pushed herself up to a sitting position, managing to mask her groan with a cough.

Quade walked into the room, and everything immediately seemed smaller. She fought the urge to cower despite believing the man in front of her would never hurt her. She gave a tentative smile and forced herself to relax.

"How are you feeling, Lexie? Do you need to rest a little longer?"

"No, I'm fine. I should get up and see about putting some bread in the oven."

"I still have to shower and change, so there's plenty of time. We can eat crackers with the soup, Lexie. You don't have to cook anything else."

"It's nothing but cornbread. You'll like it with the soup better than some crackers." She smiled and stood up.

She wasn't quite steady on her feet and swayed, but Quade was immediately by her side.

"Easy, Lexie. I don't want you to fall."

"Thanks, I'm fine." She gently withdrew from his embrace as tingles flew up and down her arms.

She hurried through the bedroom doors around the hall to the kitchen. There she found Jared stirring the soup. He looked up when she popped around the corner.

"Hey, Lexie. How are you feeling?"

"I'm fine. I'm going to make some cornbread. Quade said he still had to shower."

Quade walked in behind her and gently rested his hands on her shoulders before continuing on into the living room and the stairs. She saw Jared look at him then smile back down at her.

"Cornbread sounds good, but you we can have crackers if you don't feel up to it."

"I'm fine. I'm just a little sore in places." She smiled in hopes it would reassure him.

He just nodded but stopped stirring the soup to open the fridge and pull out a beer. She instantly looked away. She should have known that they drank. She'd have to lock her bedroom door tonight for sure. Sadness curled in the pit of her stomach. She had harbored a small seed of hope that they were different.

Lexie's experiences with men who drank weren't good ones. They grew mean when they drank. She could steer clear of them until she was well enough to leave, and then she would find somewhere else to stay. Maybe that homeless shelter Mattie had told her about.

"Hey? Are you okay? You're frowning."

"No, I'm fine. Just concentrating on what I need." She pasted a smile on her face and hurried to fix the cornbread. She needed to have dinner on the table before he had too much to drink.

Thirty minutes later, Quade came downstairs and walked into the kitchen straight to the fridge, where he pulled out a beer. Lexie pretended not to notice as she carved up the cornbread. She buttered it and placed it on a plate on the table.

"Dinner is ready when you are," she told Quade and quickly repeated it in the living room for Jared.

"I'm starved. It smells wonderful, Lexie." Quade sat down and then frowned.

"Did I forget something?" Lexie wrung her hands.

"Where's your bowl?"

"Mine? Oh. Well, I figured I would eat once you two finished. I mean, I am the cook."

"Don't matter here, Lexie. Get your bowl. You're eating with us."

"What's going on?" Jared walked in and seemed to pick up on the tenseness in the air.

"Nothing, Jared." Lexie immediately hurried to retrieve a bowl and utensils. She sat at the opposite end of the table from them

Quade looked as if he was going to say something, but Jared shook his head. Lexie was thankful for that. She was strung so tightly now, she was afraid she would burst out crying. They served themselves and passed around the plate of cornbread. She took a small piece and began to force the soup down her throat. She wanted to be out of there before the alcohol kicked in.

"Damn, this is good," Quade said.

"The cornbread is wonderful." Jared grabbed another piece.

"I–I can make some more if you need more. It won't take but about fifteen minutes." She started to get up.

"No need. This will be plenty. It's just so damn good I could make myself sick on it," Jared assured her.

"Eat up. You need it to get well." Quade smiled at her.

Lexie could almost forget her fear when he smiled like that. His entire face changed from hard and rigid to soft and open. She wanted to see him smile more often and thought about how to do it. Heat filled her cheeks when she realized where her mind had been sinking. *God!* Hadn't she had enough of the abuse? Here she was thinking about Quade in a manner that wasn't at all proper for an employee.

She took a few more sips of her soup and crammed the last of her cornbread in her mouth before standing up to clear the table. She jumped when Jared also stood up, gathering his dishes.

"Here, I have them." She held out her hands.

He hesitated then handed them to her. Their fingers touched, and a spark jumped between them, nearly making her drop the bowls. She quickly looked away as flames leapt to life deep in her cunt. God, she did not need to be aroused around them. This was insane. She barely knew them, and look what a mess she was already in, anyway.

Quade brought his empty dishes to her and dropped a kiss on top of her head.

"Dinner was delicious. Thanks, Lexie."

"You're welcome. I'll have more after I go to the grocery store and stock up. I should have had a dessert for you."

"Don't worry about it. You shouldn't have even cooked tonight. If the doctor knew, he'd have our hides for sure," Jared told her. "Come in the living room when you finish so we can talk about the grocery list."

"Okay." She swallowed and concentrated on readying the dishwasher to turn on.

As soon as they walked out of the kitchen, she let out a haggard breath. They had been nothing but nice to her. Confusion swirled around inside her. They were drinking, but they hadn't yelled at her—yet.

Lexie quickly cleaned off the table and the countertops before washing her hands and drying them on the dishcloth. She licked over her tender lip and drew in a deep breath to walk into the living room where they waited on her. She wasn't sure what to expect, but finding them watching TV in their recliners was a relief. She didn't want to interrupt them since Lowery got pissy if she said anything to him when he was watching TV.

As if sensing her approach, Jared turned his head and, smiling at her, held out his hand. He settled the chair back to the sitting position and indicated the couch next to him. The big chair swiveled.

"Come on in, Lexie. Let's talk about your job."

She nodded and quickly sat down in the middle of the couch away from either of the men now watching her. They looked at each other then returned their eyes to her.

"The list you made out looks pretty complete. You added more meat like I suggested, so I think we can safely say you covered everything. Is there anything you need to add to the list for your comfort?" Jared held the list in his hands.

"No, um, thank you, but I have everything I need right now." She couldn't help fidgeting.

"I wish you weren't so nervous around us. We'd never do anything to hurt you." Quade watched her closely.

"S–sorry. I don't know you that well."

"Well, that will come with time," Jared continued. "Tomorrow I'll go into town with you to get the groceries. I don't want you alone right now with Lowery still in town and out on bail. Plus, you're still recovering from your injuries. You don't need to be lifting heavy bags. While we're there, we'll set up an account for you to handle the household expenses out of."

"Expenses? Account? I don't understand."

"You'll be handling groceries and any other items needed to run the house. We have someone who comes in once a week to clean. You'll manage her and pay her wages from the account. It's going to take a lot of pressure off of me, Lexie. I really appreciate you're helping like this."

"Oh, I'm not sure I'm qualified to do all that."

"You'll do fine. I'll keep the books like always, so you don't have to worry about that. Just provide me with the receipts so I can keep up with them."

"Okay. I'll give it a try." She wasn't at all sure about being in charge of anything.

"What would you like to watch on TV?" Quade spoke up, reaching out with the remote for her to take it.

"Oh, nothing, thanks. I think I'll head on to bed. I'm a little tired."

Both men stood up when she did. Were they going to stop her from leaving? She squeezed her hands together, feeling trapped. They were each on one side of the couch, and the coffee table was in front of her. She had nowhere to go.

"That's fine, Lexie. I'm sure you are tired." Jared smiled at her.

She quickly looked over at Quade to see what he was doing and found that he had his hands in his pockets, just watching her. His eyes seemed to burn with intensity as he studied her. Neither man made any move toward her. She drew in a shaky breath and edged toward Jared and the quickest route of escape.

When she made it past him without his reaching out for her, she nearly cried in relief and hurried into the kitchen and around the hall to the bedroom. Lexie quietly closed the doors and locked them. She had no doubt they could get in if they truly wanted to, but it gave her some measure of comfort.

But would they really hurt her? They had only treated her with kindness and respect since she had known them. Mattie had assured her that they were good men. Still, she didn't have much luck where men were concerned. She got ready for bed wearing her favorite pajamas that were almost threadbare. They were cool and comfortable, though.

When she climbed into the bed beneath the covers, she felt so small and alone in the big bed. It was truly made for more than one person. There was little doubt in her mind now that they planned to share a wife between them. She knew that several of the people around town lived in alternative relationships. Lowery had talked about how disgusting it all was. She didn't think it was anyone's business but their own.

She settled farther down into the soft covers and closed her eyes. She needed to be up early in the morning to start breakfast. She had no doubt they were early risers with a ranch to run.

When sleep came, she found herself sandwiched between the two men in bed. They were whispering sweet, naughty things in her ears and smoothing their work-roughened hands over her skin. Jared's mouth rasped over her shoulder as he laid soft kisses along her skin. He nipped and sucked his way up her neck to pause at her earlobe before sucking it into his mouth. When he licked a long line from her jaw to her lips, she opened without thinking.

His tongue gently explored her mouth, paying attention to every detail. He slid his tongue along hers then sucked hers into his mouth to tease and tempt. She groaned into his mouth, and he released her so they could breathe.

Quade had moved farther down the bed to focus his attentions on her breasts. He massaged them with his large hands but didn't hurt her. He didn't grab at her or squeeze them hard enough to bruise as Lowery had. He was so careful, while at the same time arousing her with the way he touched them.

His mouth closed over one nipple and tugged on it with his teeth. He sucked and nipped until she was squirming between the two men. His fingers plucked and twisted her other nipple with just the right amount of pressure to send sparks form her nipples to her clit. Never had she been this excited. They each latched onto a nipple with their mouths and drew on them, sucking until she begged them to give her more. She didn't know what she was begging for, but something more than what she had then.

Just as Quade spread kisses down her abdomen toward her pelvis, she woke up with a start, panting and gasping for breath. She looked over at the clock on the bedside table and groaned. It was time to get up. She lay back down for a few seconds to regain her breath. What had she gotten herself into?

Chapter Six

Jared rolled out of bed to the smell of coffee. Quade must be up. He quickly dressed and hurried downstairs. He wanted to get breakfast started so that Lexie wouldn't have to this morning. He felt guilty that she was trying to work when she was still in such obvious discomfort.

Instead of Quade, Lexie was standing at the stove flipping bacon. She must have heard him walk in because she quickly turned around. When he smiled at her, she smiled back.

"Good morning, Lexie. I didn't expect you to be up so early."

"I figured you would want to get an early start this morning. I'm sure you have a lot to do today."

He poured a cup of coffee and watched her as he sipped. She seemed fairly relaxed compared to the night before. She had been wound tighter than a ten-penny top. He didn't know if it was just residual from being in the hospital or if they had done something to make her nervous. They would have to watch and notice what upset her so they could avoid those things. He would talk to Quade about it later in the day.

"Morning." Quade walked into the room and headed straight for the coffee. He took an appreciative sip then relaxed.

After taking a second drink, he walked over to where Lexie was taking up the bacon and ran his hand down her hair.

"Morning, Lexie. How did you sleep?"

She shivered at Quade's touch. When she didn't look up as she answered him, Jared was sure Quade noticed her unease around him. He felt for the big man.

"Morning, Quade. I'm fine. The bed is really comfortable."

"Good," he said in a gruff voice before he moved to the opposite side of the room.

"Breakfast is ready. You two can have a seat. I'll cook your eggs and serve them from the stove. How do you like them?"

"Scrambled is fine with us," Quade told her. He eased into his chair, never taking his eyes off of Lexie.

She nodded and quickly scrambled up the eggs, adding salt and pepper before pouring them in the frying pan. When they were ready, she divided them up and slipped some on each of their plates. Then she quickly broke another egg and fixed hers at Quade's lifted eyebrow.

Once breakfast was over, Quade said a muffled good-bye and hurried outside. Jared needed to talk to both her and Quade. They were dancing around each other. Both of them were obviously uncomfortable. In Quade's case, he was hurting. He wanted Lexie to like him, and she was obviously scared of him.

"I need to tend to a few things in the office before we leave. If you need me, the office is on the other side of the living room."

"I'll be ready when you are."

She busied herself cleaning up the kitchen as he headed toward the other room.

Jared didn't bother closing the door. He wanted to be able to hear in case she needed anything. He settled down to handle the paperwork necessary to keep the ranch going. Then he called a friend to let him know they were looking for another ranch hand. He promised to put out the word for him.

By the time he had everything taken care of, it was closing in on nine. The bank would be open by the time they arrived in town. He wanted to get that part out of the way first. Gathering his paperwork, Jared clicked off the desk light and headed for the kitchen to look for Lexie. He found her on her hands and knees under the sink. Her sweet bottom stuck out in easy reach. He had to curl his fingers up to keep from taking a pinch.

"Lexie? What's going on?"

She jumped and hit her head on the pipes under the sink.

"Damn." She backed out and looked up at him. "Oh, um, there's a leak, and I was fixing it."

"Honey, you don't have to work on anything around here. We'll take care of fixing things for you. Is your head okay?"

"I think I fixed it. My head's fine." She started to get up and grunted.

"Easy." Jared pulled her gently to her feet. "I don't want to see you doing something like that again. You tell us if something needs fixing."

"Okay. I've just always fixed things before." She licked her lower lip and winced.

"Promise me you won't try to work on anything again."

"Okay, I promise."

"You about ready to head into town?" Jared changed the subject because he could see that it was upsetting her.

"Let me wash up, and I'll grab my purse."

He watched her hurry to the bedroom. Then he made a mental note to call a plumber to make sure the sink didn't give her any more grief. Seconds later, she was back in the kitchen, looking freshly scrubbed. She had pulled back her hair into a ponytail and grabbed her rather old-looking purse. She needed new clothes as well, he noted. That would all have to come another time, though. He knew she would balk at his buying her clothes.

He helped her up into the truck and climbed up in the driver's seat. After making sure she had buckled in, Jared pulled out of the drive and headed to Riverbend. Twenty minutes later he pulled into a slot outside the bank.

"I'll wait for you out here," Lexie said when he started to get out.

"Nope, you have to come in and sign some paperwork. You're going to be the one signing the checks for things here in town. Plus, you have to open up a checking account so we can deposit your money in it every week."

"Oh. I guess I hadn't thought about that." She unbuckled her seatbelt and climbed out of the truck before Jarod could get around to her side.

It took nearly an hour to set up the two accounts and manage his other business while he was there. Then they headed to the grocery store. He enjoyed walking around with her pushing a cart as she checked off the items on her grocery list. She let him reach the things over her head and handle the heavier things. He even managed to get a smile or two out of her along the way.

"I think that's everything on the list," Lexie said, making a check mark by the last item they had added to the overly crowded buggy.

"One last stop. We didn't get beer." He led the way to the drink aisle and loaded a case of beer under the buggy.

He noticed she had gotten pale and was about to ask what was wrong when he made the connection. She evidently associated beer with violence. *Well, fuck.* He would have to talk to Quade about that. No doubt their drinking last night had worried her. Maybe that had been what had her so uptight all night. They would have to teach her that they didn't get violent when they drank. They rarely had more than a couple of beers at a time.

He wrapped an arm around her waist and squeezed her before letting her go. She gave him a questioning look before pushing the buggy up the aisle toward the checkout. When everything was rung up and bagged, he handed the checkbook to her to pay.

"You're going to be doing this from now on, so you need to get used to it." He smiled at her and waited by the loaded cart.

When she had finished and received the mile-long ticket, they headed toward the truck. Jared helped her up into the front then loaded the bags in the back. He had made up his mind that they would talk on the way back, but as he started the truck, he wasn't sure how to start out.

"Lexie, are you uncomfortable around Quade and me?"

"Um, I don't know you very well."

"We would never hurt you for anything, Lexie. I want you to believe that. Quade would cut off his right arm before he ever laid a hand on you."

"He's so big," she whispered without looking at him.

"He cares about you a great deal. We both do. We want you to be happy, Lexie. Try to relax around him, okay?" He glanced over at her.

Lexie was staring out the window, but she nodded.

"Okay. I'll try."

They pulled into the drive twenty minutes later and wound their way to the house. When he backed up next to the back porch, Quade walked up from the direction of the stables. He immediately walked over to the passenger side of the truck and opened the door. Jared waited to see what Lexie would do.

Quade reached in and grabbed her by the waist and gently swung her down from the truck. She had laid her hands on top of his arms when he settled her on the ground. Now she looked up with a soft smile before hurrying through the back door.

"Everything go okay in town?" Quade asked.

"Yep. Got everything set up and took care of some other business concerning that bull we're leasing."

They each grabbed several bags of groceries and carried them into the house. Lexie immediately started emptying them as they brought them in.

"She seem okay?"

"Think I figured out part of the problem. I'll talk to you about it once we finish with the groceries."

Quade grunted and walked on ahead of him into the house. As soon as they finished unloading the truck, he pulled the other man into the office with him.

"She's antsy around the beer, Quade. I think that's what had her so uptight last night. We both drank several."

"Lowery is a drunk, and he beats her. I suppose that explains it. Hell, I don't want to give up my beer, but if she can't handle it..."

"I think we just need to show her that we don't get drunk and hit her. She needs to realize that we aren't like that asshole."

Quade worked his jaw for a few seconds then nodded. It was obvious the other man didn't want to take a chance on pushing her away, but Jared figured that if they compromised too much with her they would eventually do something that would drive her away. They needed to prove her assumptions about all men based on Lowery were wrong.

"I'm going to see if she wants to see the horses after lunch," Quade said.

"Good idea. I bet she would love to see the new foals."

Jared thought that might be the prefect thing to help them to get used to each other. He hoped it worked.

* * * *

Quade stood up and took his plate over to the sink to rinse it off and stack it on the counter. She had been a little more relaxed around them during lunch. That made him feel a bit better. He swallowed down the absurd nervous lump in his throat and grabbed another glass of iced tea.

"Lexie, would you like to see the horses? We have a couple of brand new foals."

She grinned as wide as her still-healing lip would allow and nodded. Then she quickly looked over toward Jared as if for approval. It irritated him, but he schooled his expression to assure it didn't show.

"I'd love to."

"Let's get these dishes put in the dishwasher, and then we can go check them out." Quade picked up Jared's plate and carried it to the sink.

"Oh, let me take care of them first. It won't take me long." She hurried to rinse them off and load them in the dishwasher. Then she washed and dried her hands. "Am I dressed okay?"

"You look fine, Lexie. Let's go." He took her tiny hand in his much larger one and led her out the door and down toward the barn.

He eased open the door and urged her closer to the first stall where Clover and her new foal were standing. The solid chestnut-colored animal kept close to his mother. He watched Lexie's eyes light up at the sight of mother and son standing there.

"He's so pretty. What is his name?"

"Warrior. He's a fighter through and through. We had some trouble with getting him here."

"He's special, then. Are you keeping him, or will you sell him?"

"Depends on how he grows. We'll see."

The little thing eased closer to the gate where Lexie had her hand resting through the slats. He stretched out his tiny neck and tried to nose Lexie's fingers. She gasped but didn't move.

"He likes you."

She looked up at him with glittery eyes and the biggest smile he'd ever seen on her face.

"Let's go look at Ginger. You'll like her, too." He urged her farther down the walkway to where Moonglow and Ginger were housed.

The pretty little foal was nursing when they walked up. Moonglow rolled her eyes at them but continued to let Ginger nurse. They stayed and watched for a little while, and then Quade introduced her to the remaining horses in the barn. She was especially taken with Molly. The pretty chestnut filly was ten years old and a solid mount for anyone, especially a newbie. He wondered if he could get her on the back of a horse.

"Think you might like to go riding sometime? I'd love to show you around the ranch."

"Oh, I don't know how to ride." She smiled.

"Molly over there is a gentle mount. You'd be in good hands with her. I wouldn't let anything happen to you, Lexie."

"Maybe." She started toward the door.

Quade caught up with her and opened the door for her. She let him escort her back to the house with a hand at the small of her back. He called it progress and thanked the horses for setting the mood.

"I best get back to business. Thanks for showing me the horses, Quade. I enjoyed seeing them." She smiled up at him then looked down.

Quade lifted her chin with two fingers so he could look into her eyes. He loved the color of them.

"It was my pleasure. You are welcome to go down and see them anytime you want. Just don't open any of the gates." Then he slowly bent over and kissed her lightly on the lips before letting her chin go.

She continued to look up at him with a puzzled expression until he turned and walked out of the kitchen before he ruined everything and pulled her into his arms for a proper kiss.

Quade hurried down the porch steps and out to the barn where he saddled his horse and headed out to the north pasture to help the hands check fences. He hadn't bothered to bring along anything to actually do repairs, but he had tag tape to flag with if he found anything that needed fixed. His main purpose had been to get away from Lexie before he had done something to put the wariness back in her eyes.

Thirty minutes later, he was deep in conversation with one of the hands when the roar of a mountain lion snagged everyone's attention. Quade pulled out his rifle and began looking around the area, as did the other hand. They couldn't allow a mountain lion to attack their cattle. Not only did they not want to lose any cattle, they didn't want them scattered all to hell and back. Another worry that itched along

Quade's neck was that they were fairly close to the house. He didn't like the idea of a big cat being that close to Lexie.

They all searched for nearly an hour but didn't find the cat anywhere. They found tracks but no cat. Quade called Jared up on the radio and filled him in on what was going on.

"I'm going to search a little longer, but I'll be there in time for dinner. It worries me for it to be this close to the house."

"I agree, but don't take any chances. We can form a small hunting party if it shows up again or gets any closer."

"I'll be careful."

Quade had made some progress with Lexie. He wasn't about to get himself hurt before he had the chance to find out how she tasted beneath all that fear. He was willing to bet she was spicy. He couldn't wait to find out.

Chapter Seven

After nearly a week working for the guys, Lexie was finally beginning to settle down some. She didn't jump quite as often when they showed up out of the blue to check on her. She had learned that they rarely drank more than one or two beers in the evenings and had never gotten drunk or lifted a hand to her.

What she couldn't get used to was the fire that crackled around them when either of the men was close to her. Her pussy grew wet, and her nipples hardened with just a whisper from them.

Sunday morning Lexie lounged in the bed until nearly eight. She knew it was officially her day off, but she wanted to cook breakfast for them. She was sure they wouldn't stay in bed long. She quickly changed into jeans and a T-shirt before heading for the kitchen. When she walked around the corner it was to find Quade standing by the back door with nothing but a pair of jeans on. The first two buttons weren't even fastened. He was drinking a cup of coffee.

"Morning, baby girl. I didn't expect you up till noon," he said with a grin.

"Oh, um, I couldn't sleep too late. I'm not used to it. I was going to cook breakfast. Do you have any preferences?"

"It's your day off. I had some cereal already. We usually grab lunch at the diner on Sundays."

"Oh, well it seems like such a waste unless you just like going into town."

"We like to support Mattie and her family by doing business with them as much as possible. Now that we have our own personal cook, we don't go to town as often."

"I hadn't thought about it that way." She frowned.

"Hey, don't frown. We're very happy. We had already tried out one cook who didn't work out. You're a godsend, Lexie."

She brightened up again and smiled. They were really good men. She found herself growing more and more used to them every day. For the first time in a very long time, she relaxed and, as a result, was sleeping much better at night than ever before.

"I think I'm going to go down to the barn and see the horses, then. I'll see you later."

He opened the door for her but stopped her when she started to walk through. She looked up, confused. He slowly lowered his mouth to hers and kissed her. It wasn't one of the quick, soft kisses he usually gave her, either. He licked along the seam of her lips until she opened them. Then he dipped inside and licked along the roof of her mouth before sliding alongside her tongue. When he pulled back, nipping at her lower lip, Lexie opened her eyes to see his darkened and heavy lidded.

Lexie wasn't sure what to do. Should she back away or wait for him to let her go? In the end, he slowly released her and waved her off down the path to the barn. She wasn't sure what to think about the kiss. Her pussy was soaked, and her lips felt bruised and swollen, but in a good way. She had wanted to kiss him back but had been scared he would get angry if she did.

They had made it clear that they wanted her, but they hadn't forced her or even pressured her into their bed. She had found herself thinking about them on more than one occasion when she should have been concentrating on her job. What did it all mean? Could she be falling in love with them? Both of them? Lexie shook her head. She couldn't think about that right now. Maybe later after the men had gone to town for lunch she would dwell on it.

The horses had gotten used to her frequent trips there and greeted her with whinnies and snorts. She spent time with each of them but especially with Molly. The pretty filly seemed to understand her reluctance to get close to anyone for fear they would turn on her.

Everyone in her life that she had gotten close to had betrayed her somehow. Her mother had given her up for adoption when she was born. Her adoptive parents had been killed in a car crash when she had been only twelve. From there things went from bad to worse. She drifted in and out of different foster homes until she turned eighteen. Then she went to college and fell in love with Ted. He'd treated her so nice to begin with. When he graduated, he left her to marry his high school sweetheart whom he hadn't told her he was still seeing when he went home once a month.

After college, she had stayed away from men for awhile but finally allowed Johnnie into her life because he had been so insistent and patient with her. Over time, he grew possessive and jealous of anyone showing her any attention. She lost all of her girlfriends because he didn't like them and wouldn't let her spend time with them. He never hit her, but he wouldn't let her out of his sight, and while he was working, he would keep in constant contact with her, wanting to know what she was doing every minute of the day.

Finally, she left him. It had been a terrible row, and she thought for sure he would hit her, but he never had. Instead, he had thrown all of her things out the window into the street, calling her all sorts of nasty names. By then, the damage had been done, though, and she didn't think she would ever be able to find a decent man to settle down with.

Lowery had come into her life at a particularly low time. She had just lost her job at an insurance company that was laying off people, and needed to pay her rent. They had been dating for several weeks, and when he offered to let her move in with him, she had thought it a great shot of luck. Soon he became abusive, and since she hadn't gotten another job, she had no way to leave him.

She shook her head. She really couldn't trust her intuition when it came to men. She needed to be careful about letting the guys close to her. They were sure to change their minds eventually, and then she'd be without a job and a home. No, she was better off resisting them, no matter how much she found herself attracted to them.

With a sigh, she turned away from Molly and ran right into Jared.

"Oh! You startled me."

"Sorry, I thought you heard me come in."

"I guess I was too engrossed with talking to Molly." She hoped he hadn't heard anything she had said.

"She's a mighty-fine horse. You really should let Quade take you out riding one day. You would love seeing the area."

"Maybe. It's just that I've never ridden before. I'm a little scared."

"Molly is a good mount. She would be perfect for you." He stepped closer and placed a hand on her waist.

"We're getting ready to go to town. Did you need to shower or change before we left?"

"You wanted me to go with you?" she squeaked out.

"Of course. You can see Mattie again and visit with her. I'm sure she's anxious to know that you're doing okay."

"Um, okay. I should shower quickly if you're sure you have time to wait on me."

"We've got plenty of time. That's why I came to get you." He walked with her to the door of the barn.

When she would have pushed on through, he stopped her and bent down for a kiss. She was better prepared for him than she had been with Quade. But nothing prepared her for the continued fire deep inside her cunt from earlier. She had thought it gone until Jared's lips brushed across hers. She moaned when he licked at her lower lip then sucked on it. His hand massaged her waist where he held her. The tips of his fingers splayed over her ribcage.

She wasn't sure what might have happened next, but someone pushed on the door against them. Jared cursed and pulled back. Then he opened the door and nodded at the ranch hand as he escorted her out. She was sure her face was a brilliant red by the heat she felt in her cheeks.

"Let's get you to the house before I embarrass myself out here in the open." Jared's face had a tenseness she hadn't seen before.

Once they arrived back at the house, Lexie hurried into her bedroom and closed the doors. She leaned against them for several seconds while she regained her breath. Her entire body tingled from the brief contact with Jared. Heat that had still been there from Quade's earlier kiss had quickly sprung to life with Jared's attentions. Was she a slut for wanting both of them?

She swallowed down the worry and hurried to get her shower and dress before the men were ready to leave. She didn't want to hold them up and give them any reason to be disappointed with her. She recognized now that she was indeed falling in love with the two of them.

Under the stinging spray of the shower, Lexie couldn't help but moan when she brushed over her nipples with the washcloth. The raspy cloth stimulated her already-engorged nipples to the point of pain. She ran her hands down her body across her quivering belly to where her mound laid covered in soft curls. She couldn't help but think about her recurring dream of the men pleasuring her over and over. The thought of Quade's tongue at her pussy sent warm spasms throughout her body.

She ran a finger through her soaked folds to rub over her swollen clit. It would take so little to bring her to climax as aroused as she was after their kisses. She rubbed the palm of one hand over her rounded nipples again and again as she used her other hand to tease her pussy. She ran two fingers through her pussy juices then thrust them inside her hot cunt before pulling them out again.

Her clit ached for attention, so she ran a finger lightly around it several times. After teasing it and her nipples over and over again, Lexie twisted her nipple and began to press over and over against her clit. She hissed out a breath as her climax stole up on her and caught her by surprise. She quickly stuffed her hand in her mouth to stifle the scream that threatened to erupt from her mouth as she came.

It had been one of the hardest and fastest climaxes she had ever had. She blamed it on the guys. They had gotten her aroused, and then she had simmered all that time. She grinned like an idiot thinking they didn't even know how hot they made her. She would be mortified if they knew she masturbated to thoughts of them.

She quickly cleaned up and rinsed away the evidence of her climax along with a tenseness she had been harboring all morning.

Lexie dressed in her best pair of jeans and a navy blue blouse that accented her eyes. She even applied a light amount of makeup, wanting to look her best when she was with the men. She wanted to make sure that Mattie knew she was okay as well.

At a quarter after eleven, Lexie walked out of the bedroom and into the living room to find the men dressed in new blue jeans and button-down shirts. They both looked like sex on a stick to her. She wanted to eat them up. She threw caution to the wind and grinned at them.

"You both look great all dressed up like that."

"You look amazing. That blouse looks good on you," Jared said.

Quade just nodded his head with wide eyes. She wasn't sure if he approved or wasn't sure what to say. Then he bent down and kissed her on the cheek and whispered in her ear.

"You're fucking hot, baby girl."

Heat crept up her neck at his words. In that moment she felt hot.

"Let's get on the road before I change my mind," Jared said with a grin.

Lexie felt sexy with the way they were admiring her. She knew it wasn't a good idea to encourage them, but she couldn't help enjoying their attention.

When they arrived at the diner, they walked in and found a table in the back. The men sat on either side of her at the table. Mattie herself came over to take their order.

"Lexie, you look good, girl. How are these handsome men treating you?"

"Oh, they're treating me great. How did Mike do with his finals?"

"Passed with flying colors. I'll be looking for a new fry cook soon, too." She shook her head then got down to business. "What can I get you?"

They all three of them ordered the lunch special and iced tea. Several of the other patrons walked over to say hi. They all seemed to know about her. She felt herself sink deeper into her chair with every well-wisher.

"Does everyone know about Lowery?"

"It's a small town, Lexie. They all worried about you but couldn't do anything as long as you didn't leave him." Jared tried to reassure her.

When their food came, she picked at it until Quade commented on it.

"You should eat, Lexie. You need your strength, baby girl."

She nodded and tried to eat as much as possible so they wouldn't think she didn't enjoy the meal. Jared seemed to realize what was bothering her. He reached across the table and squeezed her hand.

"Honey, they all mean well. Don't let them knowing upset you, baby."

After they had finished eating lunch, the men ordered pecan pie and insisted on feeding her a bite from each of their forks. She felt conspicuous in front of half the town eating from their forks. When they settled the bill and walked out, they kept her between them on the way to the truck. Once there, Jared unlocked the door then walked around to the other side to get in. Quade helped Lexie into the cab of the truck before climbing in behind her. Just as they started to leave, Lowery's truck skidded to a stop directly behind them.

"Oh, God." Lexie buried her face in her hands.

"Shh, baby. Don't let him upset you." Quade looked over at Jared. "I've got this."

She watched him climb out of the truck and walked back to where Lowery was crawling out of his truck. The other man was obviously drunk.

"Where's my fucking bitch? You give her back to me."

"Lowery, you're drunk. You need to go home and sleep it off before you get into trouble."

"She's the one in trouble. She's fucking you both ain't she? She couldn't even keep me satisfied. How the hell she gonna take care of two of you? Bitch doesn't even know how to give a good blow job." He tried to swagger over to her side of the truck, but Quade stopped him with a hand on his shoulder.

"Don't talk about her like that. Now get in your truck and go home, Lowery. I'm not telling you again."

"What you gonna do about it, huh? You think you can take me?" Lowery shoved his chest out at Quade despite having to look up to the other man.

Just when Lexie thought there would be bloodshed, the sheriff's car pulled up. That's when she realized a small crowd had formed outside the diner. She cringed in mortification at the knowledge that everyone had heard his horrid words about their sex life.

"I've got Lowery. Quade, you can get back in the truck. I'll get his truck moved for you."

"Thanks, Sheriff." Quade walked back to the truck and climbed up next to her.

She knew there were tears in her eyes, but she couldn't do anything about it. Lowery had humiliated her in front of everyone. She swallowed around the lump in her throat and stared straight ahead. Jared still had his arm around her shoulders as he backed out of the parking spot and turned them toward the ranch.

"Are you okay, Lexie?" he asked.

"I can't believe he did that. I'm so embarrassed."

"There's nothing for you to be embarrassed about, baby girl. He was drunk. No one takes anything he says seriously." Quade clasped her hand in his, their fingers intertwining.

She didn't say anything else the rest of the trip back to the ranch. Quade's hand holding hers gave a measure of comfort she knew she shouldn't have allowed. Sitting between the two bulky men offered her security, and she longed for it to be real. She knew better, though. Men, even these men, weren't to be trusted. They would turn on you or, at the very least, change their minds.

When they pulled up outside the house, Lexie let out a breath of relief. She needed to move away from them before she did something stupid like ask one of them to hold her. As it was, she had been leaning against Quade all the way back.

He helped her down from the truck, but when she would have walked on ahead, he tucked her in at his side, wrapping an arm around her shoulders. He didn't let go of her until they were inside. Then he pulled her over to the couch and sat down, settling her on his lap. When he wrapped his arms around her, she couldn't hold back the tears any longer. She sobbed like a baby.

She was dimly aware of Jared sitting next to Quade and pulling her feet into his lap. He removed her shoes and began to massage her feet as Quade rubbed her back with one hand and held her tight against his chest with the other.

"Shh, baby girl. It's okay."

She didn't know how she would ever be able to face anyone again. She wasn't even sure how to get out of Quade's lap without having to look at either him or Jared. What must they think of her? She struggled to stop crying and sit up straight. She didn't look at either man but started to slip her feet down from Jared's lap. He let her move them, but he took one of her hands from her lap.

When she tried to pull away, Quade pulled back from her and grasped her face in his hands so that she had to look at him. What she saw in his eyes wasn't pity or amusement but something more. She wouldn't let her mind process it, because it couldn't be true. Quade couldn't love her. Not her.

Chapter Eight

"We need to talk, Lexie," Jared said.

"What about?" Her voice came out as little more than a whisper.

"About us, the three of us."

"There is no three of us, Jared. There's just you two and me." She swallowed down the worry that was beginning to eat at her gut.

When she would have wiggled out of Quade's lap, he tightened his grip. She felt his cock thicken beneath her. That stilled her faster than his hands would have. She froze, but it wasn't in fear. Her body responded to his, and her pussy juices began to leak, soaking her panties.

"I think you know that we want you, baby. We've been horny for you since the first day we met you. You can't deny that you know it. You've been tiptoeing around us for nearly a week now." Jared stood up and shoved his hands in his pockets. It only accentuated the size of his hardened cock.

"Oh, God." She closed her eyes against the sight of his obvious lust for her. Hadn't they heard anything that Lowery had said? She wasn't good in bed.

"Quade, stand her up."

Quade easily stood up with her in his arms. He let her slide slowly down his body, making her even more aware of the solid erection between his legs. She whimpered at the feel of it against her pussy, then her belly. She wanted him. In that instant, if he were to touch her, she would have gone to him. Instead, Jared turned her to look at him, and she lost sight of Quade for a minute. Jared brushed a tear away from her cheek, using his thumb. He took the tear from his thumb into his mouth and sucked, all the time keeping his eyes on hers.

"Give us a chance, baby. We want to make you feel good. We'll take good care of you, Lexie. I swear we will."

She opened her mouth to tell him that it wouldn't work, but he closed the distance and covered her mouth with his. She moaned into his while he stroked his tongue along hers, back and forth. Hers mimicked his until they were dancing around each other. When he pulled back, it wasn't to just breathe. He picked her up and carried her toward the bedroom. She saw Quade follow them from the corner of her eye.

Think, Lexie. What are you doing? They'll change just like all the others did. You'll lose your job and your place to stay. She couldn't think, though, with them so close to her. She couldn't process what was going on for the heated lust circling in her head.

Jared deposited her gently on the bed. He began to remove his boots, then his shirt, never letting his eyes stray from hers. She finally broke away from them and glanced in Quade's direction. She gasped. He had managed to remove all of his clothes except his jeans, which he was slowly pushing over his thighs right then. His cock sprang free of the confining material to bob heavily in front of him. He was thick and long and so very aroused. She licked her lips, and a drop of pre-cum pearled from the slit.

"Fuck, don't look at me like that, baby girl. I could come just watching you look at me." He kicked out of his jeans and stalked toward her.

She glanced back at Jared to find that he was also nude, with an equally impressive erection standing out in front of him. She looked from one to the other and worried that she couldn't possibly take either of them. She leaned forward and licked at Quade's cockhead to taste the dewy pre-cum. The big man hissed out a breath and grabbed her head in his hands. He didn't force her to take him. Instead, he caressed her scalp with his fingertips.

She braced her hands on his massive thighs and wrapped her mouth around his dick to suck on it. The harder she pulled against him, the deeper his nails began to dig into her scalp. She moaned around him, and he growled low in his throat. She wrapped her tongue around his stalk back and forth, up and down until he was pumping his cock in and out of her mouth. Finally, he groaned and pulled back from her mouth.

"I'm going to come if you keep doing that. I want in that tight pussy first."

Lexie pouted, her swollen lips puffed up from her ministrations. She reached for Jared, intent on getting what she wanted, and what she wanted was their cum. Jared gently held her head still as he pumped his hard cock in and out of her mouth in short, quick thrusts. She didn't mind that he held her still. He wasn't hurting her, and she had plenty of room to pull away.

Instead, she reveled in his domination. She enjoyed the feel of restrained power in his hands as he pumped his cock in and out of her wet mouth. She applied suction with each draw of his cock from her mouth in an attempt to keep him there. He groaned and pulled loose from her mouth with an audible *pop.*

"Baby, we want you. Will you let us fuck your pretty pussy?" Jared's breath came in quick hisses as he talked.

Quade was already on the bed, unbuttoning her blouse and slipping it from her shoulders before reaching around and releasing the clasp of her front-closure bra. He peeled back the cups and drew it off an inch at a time.

Jared moaned and took her breasts in his hands, weighing them then kissing them. He bent over and licked each nipple before picking one and drawing it into his mouth. He flattened it against the roof of his mouth and sucked on it until she was whimpering at the sensation.

She became dimly aware that Quade had resumed his quest to remove her clothes. He was slowly sliding her jeans down her legs now. All she was left with was the cotton underwear covering her pussy. He tucked two fingers in the waistband of them and pulled them down to her feet. He dropped them to the floor on top of her jeans.

"Fuck, you're beautiful." Quade's words aroused her even more, and another gush of fluids soaked her thighs.

The big man inhaled and grinned. Without saying a word, he slid down the bed and spread her legs with his broad shoulders. He spread her pussy lips with his fingers and buried his face in her slit, licking as fast as he could.

"Yes!" She couldn't help the scream that erupted when his tongue made contact with her needy pussy.

Jared continued his assault on her breasts, moving from one to the other. He licked, sucked, nipped, and bit until she was arching her back in an effort to give him more access. She had one arm wrapped around his head and the other reaching for Quade's, unsure about whose to concentrate on.

She thrashed her head back and forth as Quade entered her cunt with a thick finger. He pumped it in and out of Lexie, still licking her pussy juices. He ran his tongue all around her clit without touching it. She was sure he was doing it on purpose to tease her. The little bundle of nerves ached for a heavy touch. Instead, he blew his hot breath over it before ignoring it again.

Lexie growled in frustration as he continued to pleasure her pussy with his mouth and fingers. He added a second finger to her sensitive cunt and located her G-spot. He stroked it over and over until she began to moan and mew.

"Please, Quade. I need to come. Please don't stop." She didn't think she could survive if he stopped now.

Jared latched onto one of her nipples and sucked it long and hard at the same time he twisted the other one.

Quade pressed against her hot spot with his fingers while his mouth sucked in her clit and nipped at it. Fire shot from her clit to her nipples and back to her cunt. She felt as if she were on fire from the sparks going off around her. She closed her eyes, but it still seemed as if she were looking up into the sky as bright as the light inside of her. She screamed and bucked hard against them.

Neither man stopped until she was whimpering in exhaustion. Then they slowly released her, petting and soothing her with words and hands. Quade rolled off the bed then returned a minute later with his giant cock sheathed in latex. He knelt between her legs and drew them up over his arms.

"Lexie, I've got to have you, baby girl. You need to tell me to stop now if you don't want this. My cock is hard as a steel post, I want you so badly." He looked deep into her still-hazy eyes.

"Take me, Quade." It was all she could manage to get out before he was pushing at her entrance with his thick dick.

She threw back her head when he finally breached her opening with his cockhead. He thrust over and over until finally he was as far inside her as he could go. He leaned over her and kissed her lips before pulling back and rushing forward once again. His body shone with sweat as he worked his cock in and out of her climax-swollen body.

Jared lay next to her on his side, kissing her cheek and then nibbling on her neck. He whispered naughty words to her, telling her how he couldn't wait to fuck her tight ass. He swore he was going to make her come that way. He rubbed his fingers over her sensitive nipples while Quade fucked her cunt.

Lexie had never had two men at one time. She couldn't imagine what it would feel like. Now that she knew, she didn't want to go back to anything else. The dual sensations were almost more than she could handle. The effect they had on her was nothing short of explosive.

"Fuck, you're so freaking tight, Lexie. I'm going to come before I want to. Play with yourself, baby girl. I want to see your fingers playing with your clit."

She hesitated. She had never done that in front of anyone before.

"Finger your clit, baby. Quade needs you to help him out, honey." Jared's words in her ear spurred her on.

She ran her hand down her pelvis to her pussy. She slid a finger down over her pussy and felt Quade's cock enter her slit over and over. He groaned at the feel of her fingers playing with him there. Then she ran her now-wet finger back up to her clit and circled it. When she rasped over it with her moist fingertip, she shuddered. Over and over she stimulated herself until she was on the verge. She reached down with her other hand and held back her pussy lips while she pinched her clit. That was all it took. Lexie came with a squeal from that one pinch.

Her orgasm drew Quade's from him. Her pussy clamped down around his dick and squeezed the cum from his cock. Long seconds later, he collapsed over her, making sure to keep the majority of his weight off of her.

"Fuck. Aw, fuck, that was good. Baby girl, you are one hell of a woman." He rolled off of her, withdrawing his shrinking penis, and went to take care of the condom.

"Catch your breath, Lexie. I'm next. I've been waiting patiently for my turn."

* * * *

Jared brushed aside a string of hair stuck to her mouth and kissed her. Then he opened a condom packet with his teeth and sheathed his dick with it. He resumed running his hand up and down her arm as she drew in one breath after another. Finally, he decided she'd rested enough. He got up on his knees and patted her thigh.

"Lexie, baby. Up on your hands and knees for me. I want to be able to get to that pretty ass of yours."

She had rolled over at his directions, but now she looked back over her shoulder with worry in her eyes. He didn't want her scared or worried.

"I'm not going to take your ass today, baby. I'm just going to play around a little bit. I'd never hurt you, Lexie." He waited for her to relax.

When she turned back to face the head of the bed, he rubbed his condom-sheathed cock up and down her narrow slit. He rubbed over her clit once, then twice, before lodging his dick in her cunt with one quick shove. He was by no means all the way in, but it felt good to have his cockhead inside her hot pussy. She was burning him alive. Jared pulled back out and thrust in again and again until he was balls-deep inside her cunt.

"Aw, hell, baby. You are so fucking hot." He pulled out and shoved in again, hitting her cervix when he did.

She moaned. He took that as a sign that she liked having her cervix bumped. He could reach her like this so much easier. The angle was perfect for that. He squeezed her ass cheeks and pulled them apart so he could see her dark rosette. He couldn't wait to fuck her there. She would be so tight that she would probably kill him.

He looked over where Quade was lying next to her and pointed at the bedside table where he had laid out the condoms and lube. Quade handed him the lube, eyes heavy with arousal once again. Jared squeezed some out on her ass, amused when she squeezed her little asshole tighter at the cool.

"It's just lube, baby. I'm going to play a little bit. Try to relax and push out for me."

"Jared?"

"Shh, baby. Just relax."

He smoothed the lube around her little hole and rubbed the tip of his finger over and over it until it relaxed some and blossomed out for him. Then he applied a little pressure and eased his finger in to the second knuckle. She didn't make a sound and seemed to be doing okay, so he wiggled his finger around some and pushed a little farther in.

"You're doing so good, baby."

He rubbed her ass cheek with one hand then slowly pumped his finger in and out of her hot ass. She moaned for him and wiggled some, but she didn't try and pull away. Encouraged, he pulled out and added more lube to her wet hole and began to push in two fingers this time. She squirmed as he slowly moved through the tight muscular ring just inside. She groaned when he made it through. He waited for her to relax and adjust to the thickness of the two fingers before he moved them in and out. His cock was rock hard and thumping inside her at the feel of her tight ass around his fingers.

"Lexie, honey? How are you doing?"

"I'm okay." Her voice was weak but steady.

"I'm so proud of you, baby. You're doing great. Let's move around some."

He began pulling his fingers out some then sliding them back in. Over and over, slowly building speed and going deeper until she was taking them all the way up to the webbing. He began to add the rhythm of his cock into the mix until he was fucking her with both at the same time.

When she began to back up on him with each thrust of his hips, he knew she was tolerating the intrusion well. She would be fine with being prepped. Her asshole of a boyfriend hadn't known what he was doing, and hurt her. Jared and Quade would never hurt her.

"Please, Jared. I'm so close. I can't stand it. It's going to kill me."

"Relax, baby, and let it happen. You're going to fly."

He pushed against the thin barrier separating them with his fingers, feeling his cock tunneling in and out of her sweet cunt. He held her hips with one hand while he fucked her ass with the other and her pussy with his dick. She was so close he could feel the quivering around him.

Then Quade reached beneath her and began to play with her clit, and she went crazy around him, bucking and squeezing until his cock lost the battle and shot cum deep into the condom. He couldn't believe how hard he came. He pulsed inside of her over and over until he was spent. When she collapsed on the bed, he rolled them over to their sides, still joined. He was going to suffocate if he didn't manage to catch his breath soon. He could hear her raspy breath as well.

Quade's voice reached his ears as his friend soothed her. He was glad Quade thought of doing that, because he didn't think he could speak yet, let alone in a soothing voice.

A couple of minutes later, he pulled out and discarded the condom. He returned to the bed with a warm, wet cloth to clean Lexie up. She balked at first at having someone else cleaning her there but soon relaxed while Quade reassured her. The two of them made a great team for Lexie. The three of them would make a great family together.

Chapter Nine

Lexie lifted her head off of Quade's shoulder where she'd been dozing until a few seconds ago. The clock said four. It was late afternoon. She needed to get up and fix them something to eat for dinner. She had no doubt they would be hungry. She needed to think, too, and couldn't do that surrounded by them.

She explored her options on getting out of the bed without waking them and figured her best bet was to crawl down to the foot of the bed and slide off. She moved her legs and arms away from the men and slowly slipped down the bed to the foot where she carefully got off the edge. She stood still for several seconds to be sure they weren't going to wake up. Then she grabbed her clothes and dressed as quietly as possible.

In less than five minutes, she was in the kitchen fixing a pot of coffee and deciding on what to fix to eat. She decided on something simple and easy. She quickly gathered the ingredients for spaghetti and made the sauce to simmer until they woke up. She turned it down low and took her coffee outside on the back porch. She chose a rocking chair and rocked while she sipped the hot liquid. It was still quite hot outside, but she needed the caffeine to wake up and to clear her head so she could go over what had happened back in the bedroom earlier.

You're in so much trouble, Lexie. Now that you've slept with them once, they are going to expect it all the time.

Was that what she wanted? Did she want to have a sexual relationship with them while she worked for them? What happened when they were tired of her? Would she lose her job, her home?

Then there was the nagging thought in the back of her mind that she could easily fall in love with them. They treated her like a queen and hadn't raised a hand against her. She had no illusions that it could change in an instant, though. It had in the past. She just didn't trust that they were any different than any other man she had dated.

But what if they were? What if they were truly serious about her and didn't abuse her or treat her like a doormat? Didn't she owe it to herself to stick around and find out? The more she thought about it, the more questions cropped up. She wasn't really getting any closer on figuring out what she needed to do. Maybe she should do nothing for the time being.

She wasn't sure how long she had sat out there, but she had finished her coffee and was mostly just rocking when Jared walked outside with a cup. He smiled at her and walked over to lean in for a kiss. She didn't pull away, so maybe she had made up her mind to see where things went.

"How are you feeling?"

"I'm fine. Supper should be ready whenever Quade is ready."

"He was still snoring when I got up. That wasn't very nice of you to leave us in the bed together. We ended up almost hugging."

She grinned at the thought of them hugging each other and waking up. She tried to hide it but couldn't quite manage it.

"Sorry."

"No you're not. I can see that smile. I may have to spank your ass for that."

She stiffened and felt the color drain from her face.

"Hey! Don't do that. I'm not going to hurt you, baby. I'm teasing you. Haven't you ever had an erotic spanking before?" Jared had put his coffee cup down and was kneeling next to her chair, holding her hands.

"No. Spankings hurt."

"Some time, when you trust us a little more, I'll show you that they can feel really good, too. Remember earlier? I didn't hurt you when I put my fingers in your ass, did I?"

She swallowed. "Not really."

"In fact, after a little while it felt good, didn't it? Tell the truth, Lexie."

"Yes. It felt good after awhile." She couldn't deny that she had come almost as much from his fingers in her ass as from his cock in her pussy.

"Don't close down on me, baby. Everything is fine."

Lexie gave him a tentative smile and nodded. He pulled her to her feet and hugged her. Then he urged her back into the house. She immediately walked away to check on the sauce, but he followed her and wrapped his arms around her from behind. When he nuzzled her neck, she couldn't help but giggle. She was sensitive there. He nipped at her then soothed it with a lick.

"You taste like sweet nectar."

"Her pussy tastes like spicy apple cider."

Lexie jumped when Quade spoke from across the room.

"Do I smell spaghetti?" he asked with a twinkle in his eyes.

"It will be ready in about ten minutes if you can get Jared off my back long enough to fix the bread and the noodles.

"I'm hungry, Jared. Let her be for awhile." Quade's amused voice washed over her body like fingers stroking a guitar.

Lexie's nipples peaked at the sound. Jared wasn't helping matters by sucking on her earlobe, either.

"Okay, I'll leave you alone for a few minutes while you fix dinner. Then all bets are off. I can't get enough of you." He kissed her cheek and backed away.

Quade quickly grabbed her, though, and swung her around for a quick, heated kiss before he let her go. She stumbled, and both men were there holding her still.

"Sorry, baby girl. I forget that you're just a tiny thing."

Lexie harrumphed at that. She was by no means small.

"We're going to run check in with the hands. We'll be back in a few minutes." Jared opened the door, and they walked out onto the porch, closing it behind them.

With a sigh, Lexie attempted to tone down her smile and finish fixing dinner. They were full of surprises. She hadn't expected Quade to be able to be so relaxed, but it was as if having fucked her, he could relate to her better. She didn't understand it but welcomed it because she didn't feel nearly as uneasy around him now.

She had almost said "made love," but that wouldn't have been right. They hardly knew each other, and despite what she kept thinking she saw in their eyes, they didn't love her. It was way too soon for anything serious like that to have occurred.

Then what is it you're feeling for them, Lexie? Because you do feel something for them. She shook her head and sighed. She cared about them. That was all.

* * * *

After dinner, Lexie finished up the dishes and turned on the dishwasher before heading for the bedroom. She was exhausted. It had been a long and eventful day. She decided she would opt for a nice soak in the tub before bed.

Once the tub was full of hot water and she had her clothes off, Lexie slipped in the water and relaxed against the bath pillow she found in the cabinet. She closed her eyes and willed her mind to go blank. She didn't want to think about anything. Her mind needed to relax as much as her body did. They were both knotted up with tension.

Sometime later, she was half dozing when a slice of cold air sent shivers through her body. She sank a bit lower in the now-warm water, wondering if she should turn the hot back on for awhile.

"You look like a pretty little mermaid lying there in the water."

Lexie's eyes flew open to find both men staring down at her. She grabbed her cloth and tried to cover herself.

"Hey, relax, it's just us, baby. We've already seen you naked." Jared knelt on the floor by the tub and smoothed her cheek with the back of his hand.

"You startled me. What are you doing in here?"

"We came to see what you were doing. We didn't mean to upset you."

Quade sat on the edge of the tub and trailed his fingers through the water by her knees. He looked into her eyes with what looked like worry.

"I was just relaxing in the tub for awhile before I went to bed."

"You didn't come see us before you left the kitchen, and we got worried something was wrong," Quade finally said.

"Nothing is wrong. I was tired."

"We wore you out earlier." Jared chuckled.

She felt her face grow warm at the memory.

"You're so cute when you blush." Quade smiled down at her then brushed the tip of her nose with his finger. "I could eat you up when you do that."

"Nope, next taste is mine," Jared said with a laugh.

"Are you ready to get out yet, baby girl?" Quade stood up and reached for a towel.

"I better, or I'll turn into a prune."

She started to stand up, but Jared reached in and stood up with her in his arms.

"I'm getting you all wet!" she exclaimed.

"I'm about to get undressed anyway and go to bed. Don't worry about me, baby. I'd worry about what we have in store for you tonight."

"What are you talking about?"

Quade wrapped the towel around her and began to pat her dry with his big hands. He continued patting her until he was satisfied. He whipped the towel away from her before she could grab hold of it and picked her up in his arms, carrying her to the bed. He tossed her on the already-prepared bed.

Then he began to peel out of his clothes. She glanced to the side and found that Jared was doing the same thing. Did they mean to have sex again? She scrambled to her knees in the middle of the bed and grabbed the cover to shield her body.

"What are you doing?" she finally managed to squeak out.

"Getting ready for bed, baby girl."

"We sleep in the nude, Lexie." Jared finished and climbed into bed on one side.

"I wear pajamas to bed. I need to get up and get them."

"There's no need for clothes, baby. We'll keep you warm." Jared rolled over and pulled her down on the mattress again. "Did you think we would make love to you then just go back to sleeping in our own lonely beds?"

"It was sex."

"It was more than sex," Quade said quietly. "I–I care about you. That's more than sex."

"Let us love you some more, baby." Jared leaned in and kissed her.

His mouth brushed lazily over hers before settling into a deeper kiss. She couldn't help falling under his spell as he licked at the roof of her mouth then slid along the side of her tongue. They traded licks and swipes before settling into mutual tongue sucking.

When he finally pulled back, she was totally out of breath. She gasped, trying to regain it before he started something else. She knew he would. She could see it in his eyes.

He began to lick and kiss his way down her neck to her chest where he gave each breast a loving massage before nipping at her nipples and moving on. He layered kisses down her torso to her pelvis where he paid extra attention to her groin where she was very sensitive. He rubbed his whiskered cheeks against her skin then slid between her legs.

She knew what he planned to do down there. He'd already warned her she wanted a taste earlier. Still, when he licked her from slit to tip, she nearly came off the bed with pleasure. He settled down to kiss and lick and suck her juices as fast as her body released them. The more he licked, the more she made. He seemed hell-bent on drying her out. When he finally moved across her clit with his tongue, she screamed. He chuckled and began sucking on her clit in earnest until she was writhing on the bed, thrashing her head back and forth, crying out at the pleasure he was giving her.

"Fuck, you're beautiful when you come, baby girl." Quade smoothed her hair from her face and kissed her as she panted, trying to breathe.

"Don't you love watching her face as she reaches that point just before going over? She looks like she can't believe what is happening to her."

Jared licked his way back up her exhausted body and grabbed the condom that Quade held out. Then he sheathed himself and positioned his cock at her slit.

"Baby, I want you to suck Quade's cock for me. I want to watch his dick disappear into your mouth, baby." He watched her as Quade knelt by her head and fed his thick cock into her mouth.

Lexie's lips stretched to work around him. He was so large. She wasn't sure how much of him she could take, but she would try to take all of him. She wanted to please them both. They were making her feel wonderful. She had never come so much in her life. Not even by her own hand.

Jared fed his cock to her pussy a slow inch at a time as he worked his way into her tight sheath. Her cunt was swollen from coming and didn't leave him a lot of room to get in, but she knew he would eventually bury himself inside her. She needed to concentrate on Quade for now.

The thick cock took up every spare inch of room in her mouth and throat as she pulled back then moved forward. When she got him to the back of her throat, she swallowed around him and felt him jerk in her mouth.

"Aw, hell, baby girl. That felt fucking wonderful. Do it again."

She swallowed around him again and again. He reached up over her and grabbed the headboard. Then he ran his fingers around her mouth where his cock disappeared inside it. She backed off of him and swirled her tongue around him, paying extra attention to the soft skin beneath the crown. She nibbled on it and was rewarded with a hiss of breath.

"Fuck! Just like that."

She almost lost her concentration several times as Jared tunneled in and out of her wet cunt with his hard cock. She fought the urge to let go of Quade and just feel. She wanted Quade to come in her mouth though. She didn't want him to think she couldn't take him.

With that thought, she relaxed her throat and breathed through her nose and sucked him as far down as she could get him, feeling his groin hairs at her chin. She swallowed around him then pulled up and did it again.

"Aw, hell! Fuck…aw, fuck me."

She grinned and ran her hand over his balls, rolling them then squeezing them as she swallowed around him once again.

"Baby girl. I'm going to come. You need to back off, baby."

She sucked harder and was rewarded with his cum shooting down her throat and into her mouth. She swallowed over and over. Then when he was through, she licked him clean. He collapsed on the bed next to her with one hand tangled in her hair.

"That was fucking hot, baby." Jared had stopped long enough for her to take Quade's cum.

Now he pulled out and thrust back in with enough force to send her scooting up the bed. She gasped with the sensation of him bumping her cervix. It sent thrills through her body. The pleasure-pain was almost more than she could bear when he did it again and again. Then he was gilding in and out of her pussy, sending wave after wave of pleasure throughout her body. Her cunt began to tighten around him as her climax built inside. He reached down and tapped her clit several times, sending shards of sensation deep inside. Her blood turned to molten lava as she exploded again and again around him. Her spasming cunt squeezed his dick in wave after wave of rapture. She felt him stiffen and jerk inside her as he shot cum into the condom.

Jared roared out his release then collapsed over her. She wasn't sure if he had passed out or not, but she didn't think she was far behind him. She closed her eyes and fell asleep.

Chapter Ten

Lexie woke up the next morning aching all over. She felt as if she had run a marathon then jumped off a cliff. Her body was sore in the oddest of places. Then it all came back to her, and she rolled over to find that she was alone in the big bed. She looked at the alarm clock and nearly screamed. It was almost eight o'clock. She'd overslept and missed fixing their breakfast. They would be furious with her. She quickly climbed out of bed and raced to the bathroom to get ready.

After dressing, she hurried to the kitchen to find the coffee made and a note on the coffeemaker. *You looked too pretty sleeping to wake up. We hope you rested well. Don't worry. We managed breakfast on our own. See you at lunch. Quade and Jared*

Lexie breathed out a sigh of relief. They weren't angry after all. Maybe they wouldn't get that way about the least little thing. She smiled at that bit of knowledge. She could live with that.

She cleaned up their breakfast bowls where they had obviously had cereal. She would fix them leftover spaghetti for lunch. It would be more filling to them then sandwiches. She wondered what they were doing today. She thought about looking for them but decided instead to do some cleaning in her room. The maid, who came once a week, didn't go in her room.

By the time lunchtime had rolled around, she had cleaned her bedroom and bathroom and had the leftover spaghetti warmed up with fresh garlic bread. The men wandered in soon after she pulled the bread out of the oven.

"Wash up and come on. Lunch is on the table."

They smiled at her and hurried to the washroom to clean up. Then they each pulled her into a hug, stealing a kiss before sitting down at the table to eat. She smiled and sat down with them. They talked about what was going on while they ate. Then Jared asked her what she'd been doing while they were gone.

"I cleaned the bedroom and bathroom. I don't think Angel goes into the bedroom to clean."

"No, we had told her not to since no one was staying in there, but you can tell her otherwise now. We're going to move our things downstairs to the master bedroom so she won't have those two rooms to clean up anymore after that." Jared was eating as he talked and didn't notice that she has stopped eating.

"Jared?" Quade said in a quiet voice.

Jared looked up and noticed she was staring at him.

"What is it, baby?"

"You're moving in the bedroom with me? Both of you?" She wasn't sure she had heard him right.

"Do you not want us sleeping with you, baby?" he asked carefully.

"I–I don't know what to think. I guess I hadn't thought that far ahead. It's only been a week."

"We want to be with you all the time, baby girl." Quade's voice sounded odd.

"What will Angel think? The ranch hands? They will find out. You can't keep things like this a secret."

"Does it matter to you what they think? It doesn't matter to us, but they won't think anything of it. Most of the people in this town are in a polyamorous relationship, baby."

"I guess I knew that. I just don't know what to think." She could see pain in Quade's eyes, and it hurt her to know that she had put it there. "Can we maybe move your things in a few days? Let me get used to you sleeping with me."

"If that's what you want, baby. We can wait a few days. It won't change anything." Jared watched her closely as she nodded.

Quade got up and raked the rest of his spaghetti out into the trash then set his plate in the sink and walked outside.

"I've hurt him, and I didn't mean to, Jared."

"He'll be okay. He's just really taken with you, baby. He wants us to be a family, and we thought we were on our way to becoming one. It's just a setback, is all. You need more time. I understand." He stood up and carried his plate to the sink. "We'll be back inside in three or four hours. We're hiring another hand to help around the ranch so we can spend more time with you."

"Oh, I didn't realize that." Now she felt even smaller.

He bent over her chair and kissed her before walking back outside. Lexie stared at her plate for several seconds before she got up and raked hers into the trash as well. She hadn't meant to hurt Quade. He had been nothing but good to her. They were moving so fast, though. She knew in her heart that she was falling in love with them, but her mind also knew that nothing was ever what it seemed. Where would she be when they changed their minds?

* * * *

"Quade?"

"Yeah?"

"It's going to be fine. She's just scared. Give her some time to get used to the idea. We've moved pretty fast considering she just got here a week ago." Jared dropped his hand on Quade's shoulder.

"She still doesn't trust that we care about her."

"I think she does believe we care about her, but she thinks it can change. We could change our minds or just decide one day that we're tired of her. That's what's going through her head, I bet."

"How are we supposed to convince her otherwise? I'm not going to change my mind, but evidently someone has in the past."

"That's what we're working against, Quade, the past. She's been hurt over and over again, I would bet, and learning to trust is going to take time. Give her some time, Quade."

"I want to go to sleep with her in our arms and wake up to her every morning. I don't want to go back to my bedroom now that I've had that."

"I'm not planning on us doing that, but we can put off moving our clothes for a few days or weeks if that's what it takes. It's a small thing. We know the people around here don't care how we live our lives as long as no one gets hurt. She doesn't know that yet."

Quade drew in a deep breath and worked at calming his racing heart. He wanted to believe what Jared was saying, but he also knew that he loved that woman in there, and her rejection hurt more than he could have imagined.

"Okay, I'll give her some time. I know she's been hurt. That's why I know she may not ever accept us. She looks at me sometimes, and I can see where she has to work at not being afraid of me. It hurts like hell, Jared."

"I know, but I don't think she's afraid of you. She's just afraid in general. Relax around her. She's more at ease with you when you're like that."

"I'm going for a ride. I'll be back in a few hours." Quade stepped off the porch and headed for the barn.

He needed to work through his anger. He wasn't mad at her but at everyone who had hurt her. They were keeping her from being happy with them. Then there was the persistent worry that he was like his father. He refused to drink anything harder than beer, but he had his father's temperament, and it took everything inside of him to keep it under control. He worried that she had picked up on that and maybe that was the reason she sometimes looked a little warily at him.

He would never hurt her. He would walk away before she did, but maybe she could sense it in him. If she never relaxed around him, he would go crazy. He loved her more than he had ever cared about anything or anyone in his life. If he lost her, he wouldn't know how to go on.

Quade saddled his horse and mounted up. He headed for the north pastures after double checking that he had his gun loaded. He didn't want to get surprised by that mountain lion still lurking around. He rode for nearly an hour before he stopped to let his horse drink at the stream that ran through the property.

Climbing down, he noticed tracks. They looked fairly fresh. He didn't like that they were so close to the house and the barn. He decided to follow for a ways to see if he could tell where the cat might by bedding down at night. He rode for another hour and finally gave up. He still had no idea where that cat was living. It had moved from the west pastures to the north, and that worried him.

Quade turned around and headed back toward the house. He had told Jared he wouldn't be gone long. It was going on three hours now. By the time he made it back and tended to the horse, it would be close to five. He figured if Jared got too worried he would call him on the radio.

He felt a little more in control but hadn't really settled anything in his head. He still didn't like that they couldn't go ahead and move their things in with Lexie. He also wasn't any closer to figuring out how to convince her that they were serious about her. Maybe Jared was right and there just hadn't been enough time yet. He never had been good at waiting. A week really wasn't all that long to put all your trust in someone you had never known before.

When he reached the barn, he climbed down from his horse and led him inside. He was startled to find Lexie standing outside Molly's stall talking to her and feeding her a carrot.

"Oh, you're back. I should go finish dinner." She gave the rest of the carrot to the horse and wiped her hands on her jeans.

"Don't stop if you aren't ready to. I've still got to brush him down and then take a shower. There's plenty of time."

"Molly likes her carrots. I usually bring her one or two a day and talk to her. Is that okay?"

"That's fine. You're making a friend for life with her." He swung the saddle down from his horse. "Think you might like to ride her a little tomorrow? Nothing much, just around inside the paddock?" He didn't look at her as he talked.

"Um, I think I'd like to try. That is if you have time."

Quade looked up and caught her smiling at him. His heart skipped a beat then stuttered into overdrive.

"How about right after breakfast while it's still a little cooler out here?"

"Okay, that sounds like a good idea. Um, I'd better go and work on dinner. It will be ready whenever you are." She gave Molly one last pat on the nose and walked toward the door.

Quade couldn't help himself. He had to have a taste. When she started to ease past him, he reached out and snagged her ponytail and brought her to a stop. She looked up at him. There wasn't any fear in her expression, but some worry. Maybe she wasn't sure what he would do, but she didn't think he would hurt her. It was a start.

He slowly lowered his face to hers and kissed her. Tentatively at first then deeper until they were holding on to each other as if they couldn't let go. Quade backed away licking his lips. He smiled at her and let her go. She blushed a pretty pink color and hurried out the door.

He had to admit, it was a start. Maybe things weren't as bad as he felt like they were. He just needed to give her some time and keep kissing her. As long as he could kiss her, he could hold on.

* * * *

Lexie hurried from the barn up to the house. She couldn't believe she had been so wild with kissing Quade. Something about him called to her. He seemed so lost sometimes. She touched her lips with her fingers when she was safely inside the kitchen. Jared was holed up in the office, working on paperwork. She could indulge in a few minutes of daydreaming.

She sat at the kitchen table and imagined a life where they all three could live together and no one would care. Sure, the guys said they could do that now, but people like Lowery were everywhere. Then there was the fact that she knew they would get tired of her eventually and want someone else. She wasn't very pretty and was overweight. She didn't have a lot of social grace or class. She was an orphan, a give up. Somehow she couldn't see them wanting to spend the rest of their lives with her.

Why not enjoy what you have for as long as you have it, Lexie? What would it hurt to be happy for awhile?

She shook it off. Because as soon as she was happy, it would all crash down around her. She was better off being cautious. Or was she? Maybe she was being too cautious. The guys seemed so serious when they told her they cared about her. God knew she was falling hard for them. What was she going to do when it was all over? Maybe by then she would have enough money saved that she could start over somewhere away from Lowery. They had promised to help her. Surely she could depend on them to keep their promises, if nothing else. They seemed like they could be trusted in business or they wouldn't have this ranch.

Lexie felt like she was grasping at straws now. She looked over at the clock on the wall and sighed. She needed to finish up dinner. Quade would be in soon to take his shower. Just as she stood up, the back door opened, and the big man walked through the door. He smiled at her and took off his hat before heading for the stairs.

Forty-five minutes later, Quade and Jared walked into the kitchen and sat at the table to eat dinner. They were busy talking about a mountain lion and the north pasture, so she was able to watch them without having to join in the conversation. She hadn't a clue what was going on anyway. She managed to figure out that a mountain lion was stalking their cows and had moved from the west pastures to the northern one. For some reason this worried Quade. They talked about forming a hunting party one night and looking for it.

Lexie shivered. She didn't want them going out in the dark looking for a big cat like that. Surely it could attack them from anywhere, and they would never see it coming. She nearly spoke up but reminded herself that she was the cook and didn't have any say in the running of the ranch or what the guys did.

Once they had finished eating, they helped her gather the dishes then retired to the living room to watch the news and weather. She finished cleaning up the kitchen, which didn't take long at all. Then she walked into the living room and sat on the couch. Both of the men were in their recliners. Jared looked over when she walked in, but Quade hadn't seen her.

After the weather was over, she stood up to go to her room. She was tired and breakfast was early.

"Going on to bed, Lexie?" Jared asked.

"Yea, I'm about ready for bed. By the time I get my shower, I'll be half asleep."

Quade turned and smiled at her. "Don't fall asleep in the shower. You could break something."

"I don't plan on falling asleep until after I get in bed." She smiled at the other man and waved good night.

She walked into the bathroom and turned on the shower. Then she stripped out of her clothes and climbed in. The water felt wonderful pelting down on her tired muscles. She was obviously still a little stiff from the night before. She could feel her cheeks heat up at the memory.

Just as she was lathering up her hair, someone stepped into the shower with her and grabbed her around the waist when she jerked.

"Easy, baby girl. Don't fall."

"What are you doing in the shower with me?" She couldn't open her eyes because she had soap all over her face from shampooing her hair.

"I'm going to help you finish up. Here, let me wash your hair."

"You've already had a shower?" She tried again.

"Yep, that's why I'm helping you with yours."

He took over scrubbing her head, massaging it as he went. She couldn't help moaning in appreciation of the attention he paid it. Then he turned her around and rinsed her under the water. Once she was completely free of soap, he brushed away her hair and kissed her eyes.

"You can open your eyes now."

She rubbed them then opened them to find Quade staring down at her. His face held such tenderness that she reached up and ran her fingers over his cheeks.

"Thanks for washing my hair. It felt good."

"You're welcome. Let's get you dried off and in bed. You look worn out."

"I'm tired. I feel like I could fall asleep standing here."

"Well if you do, I'll put you to bed, baby girl. Just trust me to take care of you."

"I will."

Chapter Eleven

The next morning after breakfast, she met Quade at the barn, where he had Molly saddled up for her. He helped her up then led her around for a few minutes explaining the mechanics of riding a horse. When he gave her the reins and got up on his own horse, she nearly panicked but found that Molly was indeed very well behaved. She followed Lexie's lead perfectly.

After an hour, Quade called time and said she would be sore as it was, but if she stayed on much longer, she wouldn't be able to walk. Lexie was all for stopping at that. He chuckled when she stood up after being helped down from the saddle. She groaned and stretched. Quade walked up behind her and massaged her lower back.

"I'll give you a good one after you have hot bath tonight."

"Thanks, I'll probably take you up on that." She turned around and smiled up at him.

He leaned down and kissed her. It was a chaste kiss by his usual standards, but it still set her lips on fire.

"We'll ride every day after breakfast until you get the hang of it. How about that?"

"Sounds like fun. I love riding Molly. Now what do I do to take care of her?"

"I'll rub her down. You don't have to do that."

"Isn't that part of taking care of a horse?"

He smiled at her. "Yeah, it's part of taking care of a horse. Come on. I'll show you."

She spent the next thirty minutes caring for Molly and talking with Quade. They actually had a good time just talking.

"I better get back to the house and get ready for lunch. I'll see you in a little while." Lexie reached up and pecked him on the cheek before walking outside and toward the house.

After lunch, Jared called her into the office. She was worried she had done something wrong. Her hands were shaking as he sat down behind the desk.

"So, how do you feel after you first full week? Do you like it okay?"

"Um, yeah. I hope you're happy with my performance."

"Lexie, this isn't a review. I'm just trying to find out if your happy or not."

She swallowed down the lump that had formed in her throat and gave a nervous giggle. "Yeah, I'm happy. I like to cook, and this morning I got to ride Molly."

"I thought maybe since you're spending some time with Quade that you and I could spend some time together in the afternoons. How would you like that?" Jared seemed to hold his breath.

"Sure, that would be great. What did you want to do?"

"Talk. I figured we could talk about ourselves and get to know each other. Sort of like you and Quade are, only without the horses."

Lexie smiled. She liked that idea. She really hadn't even realized that's what she and Quade were doing that morning.

"So, tell me a little about your childhood, Lexie. Where did you grow up?"

She frowned. Maybe it wasn't such a good idea. She looked down and tried to figure out what she could tell him.

"Hey, this isn't supposed to be hard, baby. What's wrong?"

"Um, I grew up in foster home mostly. My mom gave me up for adoption when I was born, but then my adopted family was killed in a car accident when I was young."

"I'm sorry, baby. I didn't mean to bring up sad memories."

"It's okay. I guess I wasn't thinking, either. Tell me about you."

She listened as he told her a little bit about growing up with his two brothers and little sister on the ranch. He told her about his parents retiring to Arizona and how he and Quade became best friends.

"Wow, you had a really great time. I mean, I know it was hard work, but you enjoyed doing it for the most part."

"Yep, Quade and I built this ranch from the ground up and then merged my parents' in with it when they retired. My oldest brother is a doctor out in California, with three kids, and my youngest brother is in real estate in the East. He isn't married yet. My sister and her husband live in Oklahoma. She's got two little rug rats."

"Do you see any of them very often?"

"I see them at least once a year, if not twice. We all get together on either Christmas or Thanksgiving."

"Wow, that would be wild. I can't imagine that many people all in one place."

"You'll get to meet them this year if you stick around. I hope you will, anyway." Jared stood up and walked around to the front of the desk. He sat on the edge of it and crossed his feet at the ankles. "Think you would like to meet them?"

"I–I don't know. That's a lot of people at one time."

"Well, there's plenty of time till the holidays. Let's go over the house books. I'd like you to be able to take them over at some point, and that will leave me with the ranch to keep up with. It would help me a great deal."

Lexie felt her eyes get wide. That was a lot of responsibility for her to take on. Could she do it? She just nodded and listened as he went over the basics with her. Thirty minutes later, she called a halt.

"I'm getting mixed up. It's too much information at one time."

"You're right, sorry. I got carried away." He chuckled and pulled her into his arms. "How about a kiss?"

"A kiss? Um, sure." She reached up and kissed him lightly on the lips.

He smiled and pulled her up closer to him where he could kiss her back. It wasn't a light kiss on the lips, either. He devoured her mouth with his tongue and teeth. He licked along her lips and the roof of her mouth before sliding his tongue along hers. Then he pulled away and let her catch her breath.

"Thanks, Lexie."

The phone rang, and he got back to business. Lexie let herself out and headed back to the kitchen. It was time to work on dinner. The entire time she cooked, Lexie was thinking about what she had learned about Jared, and to some extent, Quade. Her life, by comparison, had been lonely.

When they arrived for dinner that night, she had figured out some things about herself. What could they possibly see in her? They had worked hard for what they had, and she had nothing. Her liberal-arts degree hadn't really prepared her for much of anything, and she hadn't used it for anything, either. She was a little ashamed of herself. Instead she had floated from one bad relationship to another. She needed to make something of herself and forget men. Maybe she would make a go of this job and prove to herself that she could handle the house books. Then maybe her next job wouldn't be so daunting. With the money she was making here, she would be able to set up somewhere else later.

"You're in a good mood, Lexie. How are you feeling?" Jared smiled as he ate.

"I'm doing fine. I think I'm going to need that soak in the tub, though, after my first riding lesson this morning." She smiled over at Quade. "I'm a little saddle sore."

Quade chuckled. "You'll get used to it. Put some bath salts in the water."

"Oh, I don't have any."

"I know where there are some. I'll get them for you after dinner," Quade said.

"Thanks, I appreciate it." Lexie smiled at him and continued to eat.

After she finished with cleaning up the kitchen, she headed into the bathroom to start her bath. She had forgotten about Quade's offer to get her some bath salts until he walked in on her undressing. She jumped but didn't bother trying to cover up. She was getting used to them seeing her now.

"I promised the bath salts. Hold on, baby girl." He reached up in the back of the cabinet in the bathroom and pulled out a small jar of lavender salts.

She oohed over them and sprinkled a small amount of them into the water. Quade frowned and added more.

"Won't do any good if you don't use enough." He kissed her forehead then placed the salts on the counter. "Let's get you in the water so you can soak awhile."

Lexie let him help her into the tub. He turned on the jets to the tub and helped her settle back against the bath pillow. Then he kissed her nose and left her to soak. She smiled to herself. He was such a thoughtful man. Most men wouldn't have offered, much less remembered, to get them for her. She closed her eyes and let the hot, scented water lull her into a light sleep while the jets manipulated her muscles.

When the water began to cool off, she reached up and turned off the jets before pulling the plug and climbing out of the tub. When she stepped out of the tub, Jared walked in and grabbed a towel to dry her off.

"Quade said you would probably need to get out soon. I made it just in time." He gently massaged her with the towel until she was completely dry all over.

Lexie shivered when he pulled the towel off of her. Jared chuckled and wrapped his arms around her.

"Better get you in the bed before you get pneumonia. Nothing worse than a summer cold." He bundled her under the covers and kissed her. "I'm going to take a quick shower, and then I'll be in to keep you warm. Quade should be here in a few minutes."

Lexie had finally gotten used to the idea that they were going to sleep with her. It still felt odd, but she liked it. Having both of them close to her seemed almost natural now.

Tonight, she had just gotten comfortable when Quade scooted in next to her. His cooler body sent chills down her spine. She giggled.

"You're cold. Warm up before you touch me."

"I'll warm up faster if you let me touch you." He waggled his eyebrows at her.

Then he wrapped his arms around her and squeezed until she was squealing *uncle*. About that time, Jared walked out of the bathroom and demanded to know what was going on.

"You two are like children. I can't leave you alone for a minute without you getting into some mischief." He climbed into bed and immediately began tickling Lexie.

The tickling soon turned into something more. Their hands smoothed instead of tickled as they touched her everywhere. Jared's fingers trailed lightly up her arms as Quade's moved down her legs. She began to feel warmth seep from her pussy as her juices heated up.

When Quade reached her wet pussy, he hummed his approval and began to lap up the bounty. His tongue rasped over her clit on several passes, ramping up her arousal as it did. Then Jared sucked in her nipple and flattened it to the roof of his mouth in an attempt to take more of her breast in his mouth. His other hand molded the opposite breast.

The two men were driving her crazy with their hands and mouths. She wiggled between them, unable to move far without touching one of them. They teased and tormented her until she thought she would explode in ecstasy.

Just when she was on the verge of begging them to let her come, Quade latched on to her clit and sucked until she was screaming in orgasm. He had never even used his fingers on her. She couldn't believe how easy they had gotten her to come just by sucking and playing with her breasts and pussy.

They soothed her as she came apart in their arms. Then they helped her relax after she had settled down some from her orgasm.

"Baby, we want you." Jared ran his hand down the side of her face.

"I want you, too, Jared." She looked over at the other man, too. "Quade."

"No, we want you at the same time, Lexie. Both of us in your body at once. We want to feel like we're all a part of each other."

Lexie shivered. They had played with her ass several times now. Could she do it? Did she want to do it? She realized she did want to, but she was scared. It had hurt when Lowery did it. But then he hadn't been careful like they were. She bit her lower lip and nodded.

"Yes, I want that, too."

Jared pulled her into his arms and hugged her. Then Quade had her, and she realized how good it felt to be held by them together.

"We'll take good care of you, baby. Let us do all the work," Jared said. "Quade, go ahead and lie down."

Quade stretched out on the bed and held out his hand when Jared grabbed a couple of condoms. He took his and, after opening it with his teeth, rolled it over his straining cock. Then he reached for Lexie. She cleared her throat then slowly climbed onto Quade's body. He pulled her down for a kiss.

"Baby girl, this is going to be so special. Just let us take care of you."

"I'm scared, Quade."

"Don't be afraid. We would never hurt you. If it hurts then tell us to stop and we will. I promise. Do you believe me?" He seemed to hold his breath as Lexie looked at him.

"Yes, I believe you."

"Okay, baby girl. Let's get your wet pussy on my dick. It's about to explode wanting inside you." Quade helped her position her slit over his cock and lowered her onto it an inch at a time. She moaned as he began to fill her up.

He was so thick, and she was swollen. Even her wetness from coming didn't completely ease the way. She had to pull off and push back down again two more times before she was completely seated on his cock. She sighed and began to move her pelvis around. Quade hissed and stilled her with his big hands.

"Baby girl, if you keep doing that, I'm going to come. I'm not ready to just yet." His voice held enormous strain in it.

"Okay, Lexie. Lean over Quade and let me get you ready for my cock." Jared gently pushed her forward to lie against his chest.

She felt the cold chill of the lube as he dripped it over her asshole. Then he was massaging it in with a finger. He slid easily into her back hole with one finger. It didn't even pinch. He thrust it in and out several times before pulling it out and adding more lube and a second finger. Two burned as he pressed them past the muscular ring that resisted him. Finally, with her pushing out, he pushed in with them.

She panted as he scissored them open and closed inside of her. It burned some but not real bad. He pumped them in and out of her dark hole several times. Then he pulled them out and added more lube. This time, he returned with three fingers. She couldn't stop the moan as he pressed them into her ass. They burned and pinched as they finally made it through the resistant ring. He pushed them in then stilled for her to get used to their width.

"Oh, God, it burns."

"Do I need to stop, Lexie?"

"Nooo," she moaned.

He began to thrust them slowly in and out of her ass while she panted through it. Finally he said she was ready.

"Just push back against me, baby. Okay?"

"Okay."

He removed his fingers and dribbled more lube on her dark rosette before fitting the head of his sheathed cock against her back hole. He slowly pushed in while she pushed back. The burn was tremendous. She wasn't sure she could manage it. It pinched, and when his cockhead finally popped through, the pain slowly changed into something darker. He pushed in a little more then pulled out and pushed back in.

"Easy, baby. I'm almost all the way in now."

Lexie's entire body began to shiver as he tunneled his cock deeper into her back hole. Finally he was all the way in, and she realized she held both of them inside her at one time. The enormity of the act hit her. She began to rock on them, needing the movement to still the quaking inside her.

"Easy, baby girl. We'll do the work. Just let Jared work you on and off of me."

"Please, Jared. Move. I need you to move. It's too much."

Jared pulled out then pushed back in as Quade pulled out. They tunneled in and out of her, rubbing along nerve endings that she had never felt before. The sensation of the two cocks deep inside her, moving across a thin membrane yet not touching, thrilled her. In that moment she felt closer to them than she had ever felt to another living person.

They glided in and out of her over each other through her body until sparks began to ignite nerve endings. They soon had her thrashing between them, needing more, faster, harder.

"Please, Jared. Faster! I need more," she whimpered.

"Baby girl, we don't want to hurt you." Quade sounded strained as he thrust inside her over and over again.

"I don't care. You won't hurt me. Harder, Quade. Please!"

They both began shoving their cocks in and out of her body faster and harder until stars exploded behind her eyes and fire shot through her bloodstream. She screamed as the climax rolled over her like a giant tsunami. Wave after wave caught her between them until they too came in a fiery frenzy, filling their condoms with their cum. Lexie didn't see how she would survive the onslaught of sensations and emotions that bombarded her.

"Lexie, God, baby. That was so good." Jared collapsed above her.

Quade growled below her then buried his face in her hair. "I love you, baby girl."

Chapter Twelve

Lexie's heart stuttered at his admission. She couldn't believe he had said it. Did he mean it, or was it just said in the heat of the moment? She felt tears roll down her cheeks, and then Jared was pulling carefully from her ass.

"Easy, baby. Just lie right there. I'll be right back."

Quade rubbed her back up and down and in little circles. He kissed her wet cheeks.

"Baby, we didn't mean to hurt you. Please don't cry. We wouldn't have hurt you for anything."

"Y–You didn't hurt me," she finally managed to get out. "I don't know why I'm crying."

"It's all the emotion, Lexie, baby. It's okay." Jared returned and began to clean her up with a warm wet cloth. She didn't balk this time, as she didn't have any energy left to complain.

"Baby, we love you. It's okay. We're here." Jared helped her off of Quade then pulled her into his arms as Quade went to deal with the condom.

"How can you love me so soon? You just met me a few weeks ago."

"Honey, we knew we loved you almost from the moment we saw you. It was like love at first sight."

Quade climbed back in the bed and pulled her from Jared's arms into his. He rocked her gently as he whispered how much he loved her in her ear. She couldn't get her head around their confessions of loving her. What did it all mean? Jared rubbed his hand around and around her back as Quade held her. After a few minutes, the shaking stopped and she was able to draw a deep breath.

"I'm okay now, guys. You can let me up."

"I don't want to let you up. I want to hold you all night," Quade said.

"None of us will get any sleep if you do that. Let me down, Quade." Lexie laughed.

She kissed him when he slowly let her slide off his chest. He kept one hand on her shoulder as she leaned in and kissed Jared as well.

"You're both so special. I've never felt so cared for before. I don't know how to take it or what to say."

"Don't say anything until you want to, baby. We're here. We aren't going anywhere."

"Just let us love you, baby girl, and we'll be happy."

Lexie squeezed her hand around each of theirs and let the buzz that still filled her slowly dissipate, leaving her exhausted. She closed her eyes and drifted off to sleep.

* * * *

"What do you think?" Quade asked his friend as they watched Lexie sleep.

"I think she felt it and she isn't sure what to do. We've told her we love her, and we're proving that we're not going to hurt her. It will take some time, but she'll come around. Keep spending time with her and talking to her."

"I still can't believe what you told me about her childhood. I thought mine was shitty."

"It's why she thinks that we won't stick around or that we'll turn on her. Everyone has evidently since she was a baby. They've either left her, pushed her around, or abused her. She's only been able to depend on herself all this time."

"I want to take it all away, Jared. I can't stand knowing she's hurt for so long."

"We'll take care of her from now on. She won't have to worry about anything ever again. Between the two of us we can see to whatever she needs." Jared ran a hand over her hair, marveling at how smooth it was.

He planned to ask her to marry them soon, but he could tell they needed to give her more time. She had felt the love and heard them tell her. Now she had to believe it was true. They would prove it to her every day.

Quade nodded off as Jared lay awake, listening to his snore and Lexie's little mews that she made. This was what he wanted for the rest of his life. He would fight to keep it. Lexie meant everything to him and Quade. They would make sure she was happy and safe. Early the next morning, Jared woke to find Lexie tiptoeing to the bathroom. He grinned. He would let her get dressed then join her in the kitchen. She emerged from the bathroom fully dressed not long after that. He waited for her to have time to fix coffee and rolled out of bed. Pulling on his jeans, he padded down the hall and around to the kitchen. She was standing at the back door, looking out with a cup of coffee cradled in her hands.

"Morning, baby."

She jerked but smiled when she saw him. "Morning."

"How did you sleep?"

"Good. What about you?"

"Like a baby." He reached up and grabbed a cup from the cabinet. He poured some coffee in it and took a cautious sip. *Perfect.*

He walked over to where she stood and wrapped an arm around her waist from behind. She stiffened at first but then relaxed into him. He smiled. It would take time, but she was coming around.

"You said you loved me last night. Did you really mean it, Jared?"

"Yes, baby. With all my heart."

"I'm scared. I don't know if I can do this, Jared."

"Do what, baby?"

"Love you back. I'm scared to."

"You've been hurt so many times, baby, that you're gun shy. Don't push for it. Give yourself time. We're not going anywhere."

Lexie turned in his arms and stared up at him. "How can you say that?"

"What, baby?"

"That you're not going anywhere. What happens if I'm never able to say the words?"

"I know you love us. I can see it in your eyes when we make love. It will hurt not to hear the words, but I see them and feel them when we touch."

"This all seems too good to be true. I don't know how to process it all." She sipped her coffee and moved away to stand by the sink.

"Don't try to put it in some sort of box, Lexie. Just let things happen. Don't try and push it or manipulate it. Everything will work out. I have faith that it will."

"I hope you're right, Jared, because we all stand to lose here."

"I know, baby, but any relationship is a chance. You have to step out on faith and take that chance."

"Morning, baby girl." Quade walked in wearing only a pair of jeans. He walked over and pulled her into a hug before heading for the coffee cups. "Don't forget our riding lesson after breakfast."

"I won't. I'm looking forward to it."

Jared watched them talk and smiled. They were getting along just fine. With Quade relaxing around her, she wasn't nervous around him anymore. Everything was slowly working out.

"I'm going to dress. I'll be back in time for breakfast." Jared edged his way toward the living room.

"Hold up. I'm coming, too." Quade followed him into the living room and up the stairs. When they arrived outside his door, instead of going in, he turned to Jared.

"So we wait and give her time to relax and say the words now?"

"That's right. She needs time to believe us. Right now, we've said something during sex, and she isn't sure that we could really mean it. I don't think she believes in love at first sight. She's trying, though. Keep spending time with her and give her the time she needs. As long as you're relaxed around her, she's feeling comfortable. Try not to get uptight about anything. If you do, try to stay away from her until you can get it under control."

"I found out yesterday that I'm a lot calmer around her than without her. That's bound to be good for both of us."

Jared chuckled. "Yep, you can both benefit from that. Go get dressed. She's going to have breakfast ready before long."

Quade smiled and walked into his room, closing the door behind him. Jared continued on to the bedroom on the other side of the bathroom they shared. He finished dressing, thinking back to their conversation earlier. She was really afraid she wouldn't be able to tell them that she loved them. He knew she did. It was there in her eyes when she looked at them. She loved Quade, and she loved him.

* * * *

After breakfast, Jared went out in search of the hands to go over their plans for the day while Quade got ready for Lexie's lesson. He couldn't wait to spend the next couple of hours with her. He saddled Molly and his horse then walked them out to the corral.

Several minutes later, he spied Lexie skipping her way down to the barn. He loved seeing her so happy. Her smiles were like gold to him. She approached with a giant one and wrapped her arms around his waist.

"Happy, baby girl?"

"Very. This is going to be so much fun." She let go of him and walked over to Molly with a carrot.

She talked to the horse while she fed it the carrot. Then, with Quade's help, she climbed up into the saddle and waited for his lead.

He lined their horses side by side and leaned over to give her a kiss. She giggled and pulled back afterwards. Her ears and cheeks tinged in pink.

Quade led her around the corral several times then opened the gate and led the way on a short excursion. He wanted her to get some trail time in since she was doing so well. They wouldn't go far because he knew she would get too sore if they stayed out very long. He didn't want her to be uncomfortable.

She exclaimed over every wildflower and the wild jackrabbits that would bounce out across the trail in front of them. She pointed out a roadrunner and laughed when Molly wanted to stop for a snack.

"We better turn around and head back, Lexie. I don't want you to get too sore." Quade looked around. He kept getting the feeling they were being watched.

He couldn't see anyone, but it didn't mean that one of the hands wasn't trying to stay out of the way somewhere. He didn't like the feeling, though, so he urged his horse up next to Molly. They were just passing by an outcrop of rock when he heard a low growl. *Fuck! Mountain lion.*

Quade drew his rifle to aim at the cat on the rocks above them, but he was too late. The cat was on them. It jumped, knocking them both off the horses. The screams of the horses as they galloped off jogged him from his stupor. He tried to roll over and find Lexie, but the cat jumped him. Quade fought to keep it away from his neck and face, but he felt the claws sink into skin and muscle. Then he heard Lexie's screams and the sound of a gun, then nothing.

* * * *

Lexie knew the cat's claws had gotten her on the back and down her arm, but she refused to pass out. Quade needed her. The cat was going to kill him if she didn't do something. She managed to stand up and shuffle over to where Quade and the cat where rolling on the ground. The sight of the rifle on the ground in front of her gave her hope. Surely she could hit the cat, as close as she was.

She picked it up and looked for the safety. She had never shot a gun in her life, but she knew the basics of a gun. Having found it, she slipped it off and aimed the gun for the cat. *Dear God, don't let me hit Quade.*

With them rolling around so much, she had to trust that she had the cat in her sights when she screamed and pulled the trigger as the cat turned to look at her. It yelped and flew back but limped up again. She pulled the trigger again and again until the gun was empty. She didn't even wait around to see if the cat would get up again. She threw herself at Quade, searching for some sign that he was alive.

"God, Quade. I can't lose you now. I just found you and Jared. I love you, Quade. Do you hear me? I love you!"

Quade's eyes fluttered but didn't open. She searched for all the wounds and tried applying pressure to the worst of them. She needed help, but she couldn't leave him alone. Lexie did the only thing she knew to do. She screamed for help until her throat was raw.

Finally, she heard yelling and horses hooves in the distance. Help was coming.

"Do you hear them, Quade? They're on their way. Don't you die on me." She kept holding pressure to his wounds.

Tears trailed down her face as Jared and two of the ranch hands rode up. Jared was off his horse as soon as they were close enough he could reach them in a few strides. He grabbed Lexie and hugged her.

"Dear God, Lexie. The horses came back, and then we heard the rifle shots. You're bleeding, aw, fuck!"

"Jared, I'm okay. Quade's hurt bad."

The two ranch hands were kneeling by Quade now with first-aid kits, covering his wounds with gauze and tape.

"They'll take care of him. Let me see about you. He'd kill me if something happened to you because I wasn't watching out for you. Let me see your arm, baby."

Lexie let him worry over her while she tried to pay attention to what they were doing for Quade. They had most of the deep wounds covered now. "Boss, we need to get him to the hospital. Are you ready?"

"Jared? I'm fine. Let's get Quade to the doctor." She tried to stand up but found that her legs wouldn't support her. She guessed she was trying to go into shock from the attack.

Jared picked her up and carried her over to the horse. He helped her climb on then climbed on behind her and wrapped an arm around her waist.

The ranch hands lifted Quade to the back of one of the horses, and one of them rode with him to keep him from falling off. It took twice as long to get back to the house as it had taken to get to the trail where they had been attacked. She was never so happy to see anything as she was to see that house. Her back was killing her. Jared had noticed it when he climbed up behind her and cursed a blue streak.

Once they were all safe on the ground once more, Quade began to come to.

"Lexie! Aw, fuck. Where's Lexie?"

"Easy, big guy. Lexie is fine. She's right there with Jared." One of the hands had to hold Quade down as they waited for the other one to bring the truck around the house to the back so they could load him up and get him to the hospital.

"I'm fine, Quade. I love you. I thought I'd lost you." She wrapped her arms around his head because that was about the only place she saw to touch him that wasn't bleeding.

"Oh, baby girl. I thought I'd lost you, too." He reached up and touched her cheek. Then he passed out again.

"That's probably for the best. He needs to be still," Jared said. "Come on, baby. Let's get you in the truck, too."

Lexie let Jared help her in the back. She leaned back against the seat next to where Quade lay, and the pain finally hit her. She slipped into unconsciousness.

Chapter Thirteen

Quade woke in slow increments, feeling like his body was on fire from a thousand tiny needle pricks. What in the hell had happened to him? He struggled to remember for a few seconds, and then it all came back in a blinding flash.

"Lexie!"

"Shh, Quade. You'll wake her up. I just got her to sleep."

"Is she okay? The damn mountain lion attacked us."

"I know. She shot that thing and saved both of your lives."

"She shot it?" Quade couldn't quite believe it.

"She still can't believe she missed hitting you."

"I'll be damned. Fuck, I feel like a porcupine got ahold of me."

"You've got damn near a hundred stitches in your body, man. That cat did some damage. Thank God none of it was internal. You're arms took the brunt of it." Jared leaned against the railing of the hospital bed.

"But Lexie is okay."

"She got some scratches, too, but only a few and not as deep as yours. She said the cat got her when it knocked you off the horses."

"I heard her say she loved me. Did she really say that?"

"Yeah, she really said it, Quade. She told me she loved me, too."

"How long before she wakes up? I want to hear her say it again."

Jared chuckled. "It's only been about twenty minutes. Give her some time, man. She hadn't been asleep since she woke up on the trip to the hospital."

"Did the doctor say how long until I can get out of here?"

"He's giving you some IV medications. If you don't run a fever overnight, you can go home tomorrow afternoon. Lexie, too. She's in the room next to you. I had to let her come over here, or she would have had us all thrown out."

"She can be a little spitfire, can't she?"

"She's our little spitfire, though." Jared grinned down at him. "I plan on asking her to marry us just as soon as you both are all healed up. I think she's ready."

"Hot damn!"

"Quade?" Lexie opened her eyes. She was lying on the recliner by the hospital bed.

"Hey, baby girl. I didn't mean to wake you up."

"Jared! Why didn't you wake me up? He's awake." She started trying to climb out of the recliner.

"Whoa, baby. You'll pull out your IV if you aren't careful, and then that nice nurse will make you stay in your room." Jared untangled her IV line and helped her sit up on the edge of the chair so she could reach Quade's arm.

"I don't know where to touch you, Quade. You're hurt so badly."

"It's not that bad, Lexie. I'll heal in no time. I'm so sorry you got hurt. I never should have taken you out there until we'd killed that mountain lion."

"It wasn't your fault, silly. It could have happened any time we went out riding. It could have happened when I was out walking in the yard. I'm just so glad you're going to be okay. I was so worried."

"I love you, baby girl."

"I love you, Quade. I love you so much! I don't know what I would have done if I had lost you."

Just then a nurse walked in with medication. She frowned at them.

"I didn't realize you were going to let her stay this long when I said she could visit."

"She's stubborn. It was either let her stay over here or listen to her complain and get no sleep."

"Jared!"

The nurse chuckled and handed her some medication. Then she helped Quade with his. She fussed over his bandages, making sure they were all still intact before winking at him and leaving.

"She was flirting with you, Quade." Lexie grinned. "She just doesn't know it, but you're mine."

"I know I'm yours, baby girl. Don't you worry."

"The doctor said it would be seven days before they would take the stitches out of us. We have to be still and not pull on them. What are we going to do for seven days, Quade?"

"Hmm, I think I could use some down time with my baby girl in my arms. I'm sure we can watch TV together while we run poor Jared crazy getting us something to eat and drink."

"Don't bother planning over there. You're not driving me crazy. I'm going to be right there on the other side of you, Lexie. We'll all take some time off. I'll hire someone to come cook for us while we're stuck in bed."

Lexie grinned then frowned. "But cooking is my job, Jared."

"Not until you're well, baby. Then you can go back to cooking. Don't worry. No one is taking your place."

She nodded, but Quade realized that she wasn't so sure. He winced. They needed to figure out a way to reassure her that she had a permanent place in their lives sooner rather than later. Maybe Jared needed to propose as soon as they got home. He didn't want her worrying. He would talk to him about it when Lexie was asleep again.

Quade reached out with his hand and tried to rub Lexie's hand, but his was so wrapped up, he couldn't really feel what he was doing. Aggravated, he closed his eyes and worried. If she thought they didn't need her anymore, she might try to leave. He was afraid they wouldn't even realize it until it was too late.

"Quade? You asleep?" Jared asked quietly after awhile.

"No."

"Lexie is asleep again. I'm going to go put her in her bed, so she'll rest better. I'll be back to check on you in a few minutes."

"Be sure and come back. We need to talk about something."

Jared looked at him with a frown and nodded. "I'll be right back."

He watched as Jared picked Lexie up and maneuvered her IV pole through the door and out into the hall. He quietly closed the door behind them.

Quade waited for nearly fifteen minutes before Jared returned.

"Sorry, but she woke up, and I had to convince her to stay and go back to sleep. She's resting, but I don't want to leave her alone too long."

"No, she's likely to get up and walk over here on her own if you aren't careful."

"What did you need to talk with me about?"

"I think that little quip about hiring someone to cook for us scared Lexie. We need to be sure she knows she's permanent. I think you need to ask her to marry us as soon as we get home. I'm scared she's going to get nervous and leave, Jared."

"Hell, I didn't think about that. I just want her to rest and not do anything while she's healing up. You both need to be still and quiet until those stitches come out. We sure don't want them infected or pulled out."

"You need to have everything ready so she can't say no. The ring is in the vault, right?"

"Yes, and I was thinking we would plan the civil marriage for winter, but maybe we need to do that as soon as we can get a marriage license." Jared stuck his hands on his hips. "Will you feel like standing up with me in a couple of weeks?"

"The sooner the better. I'll prop myself up if I have to. I don't want her to get cold feet and leave."

"Don't worry, Quade. I'm going to make sure she stays with us forever."

* * * *

Two days later, Lexie woke up next to Jared in their bed. She reached for Quade and didn't find him. Worried, she slipped out of bed and grabbed her robe. She stepped into her house shoes and eased downstairs to find Quade sitting in one of the recliners, dozing. Unsure what to do, Lexie decided to fix some coffee. She would take him some and find out why he wasn't in bed with them.

Once the coffee was made, she carefully carried two cups into the living room. She set one of them down on the end table and sat on the arm of the recliner with the other.

"Quade?"

"Hmm?" He opened his eyes and smiled at her. "Hey, baby girl. What are you doing up?"

"I fixed you some coffee." She helped him sip some of it. Then she sat it down next to hers. "Why are you out of bed, Quade? Did I hurt you in the middle of the night?"

"No, you didn't hurt me. I was restless and couldn't sleep. Thought I would come down here so I wouldn't wake you and Jared up."

"Why are you restless? Is something bothering you? Are you hurting too much to rest?"

"I'm fine, Lexie. I'm just not used to being in bed so much."

"I missed you up there. I want to crawl up into your lap, but I'm afraid I'll hurt you."

"Come on up, baby girl. You won't hurt me. I'll keep my arms out of the way."

Lexie took a sip of her coffee then crawled up from the edge of the recliner until she was sitting back in Quade's lap. She sighed. It felt so good to be in his arms again. Even if it meant she couldn't feel them around her yet.

"There you two are. I wondered where you had gotten off to." Jared descended the stairs into the living room. "I smell coffee."

"There are two cups over here if you want one of them." Lexie pointed at them on the end table.

"Sounds good. I'll fix us something to eat in a few minutes. What's your preference, Lexie, baby?"

"Before you answer that, Lexie, you need to know that he can't cook worth anything."

"I can do omelets." Jared frowned.

"Omelets sound good to me." Lexie laughed.

"Jared? Maybe now would be a good time."

"Now? Are you sure?"

"Yeah."

"What are you two talking about?"

"Just a minute, Lexie. I'll be right back."

Lexie watched him hurry around to the office. He was gone for several minutes before he came jogging back into the room. She looked at Quade and frowned. He had a huge grin on his face. *What is up with them?*

Jared got on his knees next to the recliner and took her hand.

"Lexie we love you with all our hearts and all our souls. We want to spend the rest of our lives with you. Will you do us the honor of being our wife?" He opened his hand, and lying in it was a beautiful diamond solitaire that had to be three carats.

Lexie's eyes swelled with tears. She looked from one man to the other and burst out crying.

"Oh, baby girl. What's wrong? Don't cry."

"I can't help it. I don't know what to say. I love you both so much, but are you sure? I'm nothing special. You might get tired of me, then what?"

"Lexie, look at me." Jared cupped her cheeks in his hands. "We both love you. We're not going to change our minds. You are perfect for us. We think we're perfect for you, too." He smiled.

"Please say yes, baby girl. I don't think I can stand it if you say no."

Lexie smiled and nodded her head. She leaned in and kissed first Jared then Quade. She loved them with all her heart and soul. Surely they could make it work. Others in the area lived in ménage relationships. If it worked for them, it would work for her, Quade, and Jared as well.

"I can't believe this. I'm actually going to get married." She stopped and frowned. "Which of you do I really marry? How does this work?"

"You'll marry me," Jared said. "I'm the oldest, and some of the land is in my name, so it will go to you should something happen to me. Then we'll all say vows in a private ceremony with some close friends later."

"I can't wait to marry you both. When do we get married?"

Jared chuckled. "I thought next week. We need to get the stitches out and get the marriage license as well. Then we'll come back here for the private ceremony. What do you think?"

"Sounds good to me. I'll need to get a dress, though. I don't have one."

"We'll get you one. Don't worry about it. Right now the only thing you need to worry about is getting well. You and Quade both. I'll take care of all the details."

"I can't wait to see you two all dressed up with your cowboy hats on and dress clothes. You'll both look so handsome."

"I don't know about that, baby girl. My arms are going to look pretty bad."

"They'll be fine. You're lucky to be alive."

"Enough procrastinating. Let's see if this fits. I want to see you wearing our ring, baby," Jared said.

Lexie held out her hand and let Jared slip it on her left hand. It fit like it was made for her. She looked at it and started crying all over again.

"She's crying again, Jared. Do something." Quade frowned.

"I'm sorry. I can't help it. I'm so happy. I never dreamed I would ever find anyone to love me like the two of you do, and I found two of you!"

"I'm going to fix us some breakfast. You two need to eat to heal. Then I'm going to run to town and start the ball rolling on getting things ready for our wedding. You'll have to go with me next time, Lexie, to get the license." Jared stood up and ruffled Lexie's hair.

"Do you need my help?" She really didn't want to move, but if Jared needed help in the kitchen, she would help.

"Nope. I can handle a few omelets, baby. Just keep Quade happy, and I'll bring them to you in a little while.

Lexie hoped she could keep both of them happy. She looked at the ring and let it sink in that she had a home now and two someones who loved her. Life couldn't get any better than this.

Chapter Fourteen

"Are you sure you feel up to going today, baby?" Jared asked.

"I'm fine. The stitches are out, and I need to get a dress for the wedding. I don't want to look bad for my own wedding."

"You could never look bad, Lexie. You're the most beautiful woman I've ever seen."

Lexie rolled her eyes but squeezed his hand as they walked down the sidewalk of Riverbend. She looked in the different stores and realized she hadn't really ever shopped in the town before. They had a lot of small boutiques she would like to explore one day.

Finally they reached the store that Mattie had told them about. It carried fancy dresses. She stepped inside the shop and immediately decided the place was too expensive for her. She started to turn around, but Jared stopped her.

"Whoa. Where are you going?"

"I can't afford these dresses, Jared. I need to find a different store."

"Honey, you can afford anything you want. Quade and I can afford to buy you everything you want. Just point to it and it's yours."

"I can't take your money, Jared. This is my wedding dress. I have to buy it," she whispered under her breath.

"Nonsense. You find what you like, and we'll take it out of your salary from last week. How's that?"

Lexie thought about it and nodded. "That will work."

"Now get in there and find a pretty dress for me." Jared gave her a gentle push into the main part of the store.

Lexie felt self-conscious surrounded by so many pretty dresses. A saleslady walked up and asked if she could help her.

"I'm looking for a simple dress for my wedding. Nothing fancy, really. I was thinking about something in a pale mint or maybe blue."

"I've got several nice things I think you will like." The saleslady drew her deeper into the store and showed her several very pretty dresses.

She tried on several and finally picked a soft mint-green dress that looked great on her rounded figure. She also got shoes to match and a pair of lacy underwear. She couldn't wait for the guys to see her in nothing but her garters and lacy bra and panties. She let the saleslady wrap everything up and charge it to Jared. She felt bad about doing that, but she had no money to her name outside of her wages for the last week.

Once again, Lexie worried that she wasn't bringing anything to the marriage outside of her ability to cook. She had nothing to show for her life. She pushed it aside, determined not to let her low self-esteem ruin her upcoming nuptials.

When she walked out of the shop with her purchases, she expected to see Jared sitting in the truck or standing outside of it. Instead, she was alone. She shrugged and hung the dress in the backseat of the truck while she waited for Jared to return. He probably saw something or someone and got distracted.

"You think you've got them wrapped around your finger, don't you, bitch? They'll get tired of you like I did soon enough." Lowery walked up and pointed at her.

"Leave me alone, Lowery. You're not supposed to be anywhere around me." Lexie looked around frantically for Jared or someone else to help her.

"You owe me for taking care of your lazy ass all that time. I worked to put a roof over your worthless head. You didn't have nothing till I took you in. Do they know how you sponged off of me when you didn't have anything? That's what you're doing now with them. You're just using them to get what you want. All of you women are the same."

"That's not true, Lowery. I worked hard while we were together. I didn't sponge off of you."

"Not after I put my foot down about you getting a job. I bet they don't know how lazy you are, do they? Maybe I should tell them about what they're getting themselves into."

"Lexie? Are you okay, baby?" Jared walked up and wrapped his arm around her. "Lowery, you're not supposed to be within fifty feet of her."

"You should really learn a little about that bitch you're saddling yourself with. She's just a lazy tramp. She takes up with whoever will pay her bills for her. I got stuck paying her way. You will, too."

"Shut the fuck up, Lowery, before I call the sheriff on you."

"I'm just telling you for your own good. You can't trust her. She'll use you like she used me."

Jared pulled out his phone and started dialing the sheriff's office. Lowery looked back and forth up the street before running off.

"I'm sorry, baby. I shouldn't have left the store. I wanted to get a surprise for you and didn't think about Lowery showing up."

"It's okay. But, Jared, it's not true. I didn't sponge off of him. I worked. I'm a hard worker."

"Shh, baby. You don't have to try and convince me of anything. I know you're a hard worker."

"What if he tells everyone all of those lies? Then everyone will think I'm marrying you for your money."

"Everyone knows better, baby. They all know Lowery is a drunken bastard who hits women. No one will believe anything he says."

"I'm ready to go home, Jared."

"Let's go, baby. Quade will be happy to see you."

Jared helped her up in the truck then drove them home. As soon as they parked, Lexie was out of the truck and grabbing her packages.

"Here, baby. I'll get those and put them up for you. You go attack Quade. He's probably tired of his own company by now."

Lexie didn't need to be told twice. She ran through the house until she found Quade sitting on the back porch.

"There you are! I was looking for you everywhere. What are you doing out here?"

"Waiting for you to get back, baby girl. I missed you."

"I missed you, too." She climbed up in his lap and wrapped his scarred arms around her.

"Did you get a pretty dress for me?"

"I got a very pretty dress, but you can't see it till the wedding."

"Did you get all the paperwork done?"

"Everything's ready for the wedding now. All you have to do is show up dressed in your dress clothes and your cowboy hat. I want the cowboy hat for sure, Quade."

Quade chuckled. "I hear you, baby girl. I'll wear my hat."

"I'm tired, Quade. Want to take a nap?"

"Hmm, a nap, you say?"

"Yeah, I'll bet Jared would take one with us."

"I think I can be persuaded to take one just for you, baby girl."

Quade helped Lexie climb out of his lap before standing up. They walked back inside and found Jared in the office working on the computer.

"We decided we need a nap. Don't you want to take one with us?" Lexie asked.

Jared looked up and grinned at them. "I'm sure we all need one."

The three of them climbed the stairs together to the second floor. Lexie was the first one in the room. She immediately began stripping. She stopped and helped Quade with his jeans and then climbed up on the bed where she sat waiting for her men.

When Quade and Jared were both nude, they advanced on Lexie and attacked her in the bed. Jared immediately went for her breasts. He honed in on a nipple with his mouth. Sucking it in, he teased it with his tongue before nipping at it with his teeth. Then he changed over to the other breast and treated it to the same exquisite torture.

Quade kissed and licked his way down her belly to her pussy. He nuzzled her there before he moved over and kissed her inner thighs. She squirmed, wanting him to lick her clit. She was already aroused and needy.

Instead of her clit, Quade concentrated on her pussy lips. He sucked and licked them clean before moving to stab her cunt with his stiffened tongue. She groaned and tilted her pelvis, hoping to encourage him to seek out her clit. He knew what she was doing, though, and chuckled.

"Easy, baby girl. I'll take care of you, but I'm not ready yet. I want more of your sweet cream."

"Oh, Quade, please don't tease me." She reached for him but couldn't reach him with Jared in the way.

Both of her men were driving her crazy. Jared with his hot mouth and Quade with his wicked, teasing tongue. She moaned as heat built in her womb. Little electrical sparks traveled from her pussy to her nipples and down her spine. She was close but needed more. She knew they wouldn't give it to her until they were ready.

"Please, Jared. Please make me come."

Jared nipped at her nipple then chuckled. "Talk to Quade, baby."

"Quade." She rocked her pelvis again.

After stabbing her pussy with his tongue several more times, Quade rasped his tongue over her clit until she screamed in climax. Before she had even begun to come down from the glorious high, he was sheathed and pushing into her pussy with his throbbing cock. Another thrill of climax settled into her cunt as he shoved forward trying to fill her pussy with his dick.

Just as she began to settle into Quade's rhythm, Jared twisted her nipples. It sent another spark through her body. She screamed and came again as Quade plunged inside her welcoming pussy over and over. When he pulled out without coming, Lexie whimpered.

"What's wrong?"

"Nothing, Lexie. I want all of us to be together again. I'm just going to change positions."

She smiled and looked up at Jared. He hadn't wanted to try it again so soon after the attack, but Lexie was ready. She climbed up on top of Quade and eased down on his thick dick. Her breath came out in a long hiss as she swallowed his cock in her cunt. Then Jared was behind her, pressing her back to get her to lay forward.

"Easy, Lexie. Remember to push out each time I enter you."

She felt the cold gel of the lube drop on her back hole before Jared's warm finger began massaging it inside her little rosette. He pushed in two fingers past her resistant ring with only a mild burn. Pumping them in and out, he loosened her hole for his waiting cock. Then he pulled out and added more lube. This time he entered her with three fingers. They burned something fierce but soon made it through the tight ring. She breathed a sigh of relief when he was past it.

"Okay, baby. You're ready. Push out for me."

She followed his directions as he slowly entered her ass, spreading her cheeks wide as he did. The pain was there but soon turned to a sweet burn as he made it in with a pop. She moaned and wiggled her butt until he started pumping his cock through her back tunnel. Quade pulled out then pushed in as Jared tunneled his way in and then back out.

Nothing compared to having both her men inside her at one time. She lit up all over from the intense pleasure of their constant friction over the thin membrane separating them. Her cunt began to contract as her ass spasmed around them. She was going to come, and they were still speeding up. God, but it felt so good.

"I'm not going to last, baby girl. You're pussy is so fucking tight. I can't hold off." He slipped his hand between them and pressed on her clit. Lexie hollered out, too hoarse to scream again. She called out their names over and over as her climax sent her flying to the stars. Lights flashed behind her eyelids as she soared into the sky.

Somewhere in the back part of her brain it registered that her men had come as well as they each called out her name. She smiled. This was what home was, loving her two cowboys and trusting them to take care of her. Lexie closed her eyes and slipped off to sleep.

Epilogue

Lexie stood in the courtroom as the judge walked in. Jared and Quade stood on either side of her. With them at her side, she didn't fear Lowery like she had. He couldn't do anything to her now.

Once the judge was sitting, the entire assembly could sit down as well. She waited anxiously, ready for it all to be over. She was ready to get on with her life. Putting Lowery in jail would seal the past for her. Then her upcoming wedding would be a guaranteed success.

She had it all planned right down to the words of promise she would say. They were having a private ceremony just for friends and family. It was then that she would pledge her love and honor to Jared and Quade as was traditional in the little town of Riverbend. Far be it for her to break with tradition.

The attorney for Lowery called his first witness. This continued until the judge put a stop to it. It was obvious they had dug up all sorts of riff raff to testify to Lowery's good name and character.

Then it was her lawyer's turn. He called her to the stand, and she told of the two years she had been with Lowery and his treatment of her. Then she told about the last time he'd beaten her up. She couldn't stop the tears from falling as she described the pain she had been in.

Her lawyer called the sheriff as well as everyone from the diner. When he called her fiancés, Lowery began to protest, saying it was immoral for them to testify. The judge charged him with contempt of court and had him taken away. The trial was continued without him.

When the judge sentenced him to five years for domestic valance and aggravated assault, Lexie was disappointed but had been expecting it. Her lawyer had explained that since he didn't have a past history of judicial cases, there was a good chance that he would be let off with a slap on the hand. So maybe she should be content with the sentencing. It sucked, but he was also ordered to stay out of Riverbend for the rest of his life.

"How do you feel about it, Lexie?" Quade asked.

"I'm okay with it. We didn't expect him to face any jail time at all. If he never shows his face here again, then it will be fine."

"If he ever does, Jared and I will personally see that he never comes back."

Lexie grinned and hugged him. He was a big man, and she couldn't wrap her arms around him. Still she always tried. Then she grabbed Jared and did the same to him.

"I love you both so much."

"We love you, too. Let's go."

"How about some apple pie from the diner?" Quade was always hungry.

She grinned up at him. "How about I cook an apple pie right after our nap?"

"Nap?" Quade grabbed her by the wrist and almost made her jog to keep up with him as he drew her toward the truck.

"Where are you going, Quade?" Jared demanded as he followed them.

"Home, for a nap," Quade said.

"A nap? I'm in!"

Once they arrived at the truck, she started to get in the truck but was hauled up against the side of the truck and a knock-your-socks-off kiss was planted on her mouth.

"What was that for?" She giggled out loud.

She wasn't about to interfere with Quade when he was on a mission. The man had a one-track mind that changed easily. Now that she'd suggested the word *nap*, he had a new agenda on his brain. Get her home as fast as he could. "Nap" to them was a code word for dirty, raunchy sex.

She smiled when he assaulted her mouth before shoving her inside the truck. She was dimly aware that Jared had climbed into the truck on the other side of her. Her head was spinning from the kiss.

When Jared pulled her closer to him, she went willingly. He covered her face and neck with kisses. She kept looking at her soon-to-be husbands, hardly believing her good luck. When all else had looked bleak in her life, they had swooped in and saved her from Lowery and from herself. How could she do anything but trust her cowboys?

THE END

WWW.MARLAMONROE.COM

ABOUT THE AUTHOR

Marla Monroe lives in the southern part of the United States. She writes sexy romance from the heart and often puts a twist of suspense in her books. She is a nurse and works in a busy hospital but finds plenty of time to follow her two passions, reading and writing. You can find her in a book store or a library at any given time.

Marla would love for you to visit her at her blog at themarlamonroe.blogspot.com and leave a comment. Or you can reach her at her by e-mail at themarlamonroe@yahoo.com.

Also by Marla Monroe

Ménage Everlasting: Riverbend, Texas Heat 2: *Beth's Little Secret*

For all other titles, please visit
www.bookstrand.com/marla-monroe

Siren Publishing, Inc.
www.SirenPublishing.com

Lightning Source UK Ltd.
Milton Keynes UK
UKOW06f1903121017
310896UK00009B/123/P